WHATEVER HAPPENED TO INTERRACIAL LOVE?

WHATEVER HAPPENED TO
INTERRACIAL LOVE?

STORIES

KATHLEEN COLLINS

"Interiors" was first published in *A Public Space,* Fall 2015.

WHATEVER HAPPENED TO INTERRACIAL LOVE? Copyright © 2016 by The Estate of Kathleen Conwell Prettyman. Foreword © 2016 by Elizabeth Alexander. All rights reserved. Printed in the United States of America. No part of this book may be used or reproduced in any manner whatsoever without written permission except in the case of brief quotations embodied in critical articles and reviews. For information, address HarperCollins Publishers, 195 Broadway, New York, NY 10007.

Designed by Ashley Tucker

ISBN 978-0-06-248415-4

It is easy to do evil things,
easy to harm oneself.
To do what is good,
what is good for oneself,
is very difficult.

—KATHLEEN COLLINS

CONTENTS

ACKNOWLEDGMENTS

Many thanks to Brigid Hughes, the prescient editor of *A Public Space*, without whom this collection would likely never have seen the light of day.

FOREWORD: IN SEARCH OF KATHLEEN COLLINS

I first heard of Kathleen Collins when I was in graduate school in the mid-1980s. I was studying English with a focus on African American and Caribbean literature. The black cultural feminism I encountered in books, fellow students, and an ever-expanding elsewhere of writers and intellectuals was teaching me how to think. The study of the ideas of black women also taught me that we would not, should not, find all we needed in the classroom. We needed to be autodidacts; we needed to pass books from hand to hand; we needed to search, and thus be inspired by hard-won effort to create ourselves. We needed to understand that there is power in searching and finding and not having things handed to us. We would follow June Jordan's declaration in "Poem for South African Women": "We are the ones we have been waiting for."

The black women's voices that were front and center for us in the 1980s came mostly in the forms of poetry and the novel. The year 1970 had been a watershed year for black women's literature, as it heralded first-book publications by the likes of Toni Morrison, Alice Walker, and Toni Cade Bambara. Gwendolyn Brooks, Sonia Sanchez, and Lucille Clifton shone brightening lights, and Rita Dove was a comet on the rise. The criticism of polymaths Audre Lorde and June Jordan and Sherley Anne Williams—poet-critics all—provided theoretical guidance. And scholars such as Deborah McDowell, Valerie Smith, Barbara Smith, Barbara Christian, Sylvia Wynter, Thadious Davis, Eleanor Traylor, Cheryl Wall, and Hortense Spillers, among others, were teaching us how to make sense of this moment we were in and vision the unwritten future.

In school I was acutely aware of who was and wasn't teaching me, learning to read silence and omission. Black feminist studies taught me that. Our oral and written exams did not include work being made in the burgeoning moment, but one of the many tectonic plate–shifting excitements of the time was the understanding that the contemporary was something that we could include in our work.

That was the written word. Just as exciting was the

black cinema boom, the second wave that Spike Lee marked to widening audiences and that included Julie Dash, Haile Gerima, Bille Woodberry, Charles Burnett, and so many others. That was the context in which I first heard of Kathleen Collins, and her legendary film *Losing Ground*.

How I longed to see *Losing Ground*. A film made by a black woman, whose subject was—what?—a black woman philosophy professor? With a painter husband? Whose black intellectual artistic life I was trying to live myself? And, oh, these people were funny, too? In the 1980s of course we couldn't get things streamed online. We couldn't watch films on our laptops. It would be many, many years before I would have the revelatory experience of seeing *Losing Ground* and encountering this extraordinary black female protagonist who was dazzlingly familiar to me. She would be living a complex black and Puerto Rican life, a New York life. She would have a palpably infinite inner life. She would be shown teaching, in the classroom, expounding on actual ideas and encouraging her students—who adored her—to do the same. The erotics of thinking would pulse from the screen. Her marital tensions would take place entirely outside "the white gaze." Oh, and did I say everyone in the movie would be beautiful, in the quotidian way of black people who are lit from within by the power of living in the free zone of ideas and creativity?

Now, reading *Whatever Happened to Interracial Love?* is like finding Kathleen Collins Atlantis once again. It was enough to search for the film, to unearth that legacy. But to also see that she had cast her ideas in the short-story form—and to encounter with a start her singular, sophisticated black and white bohemians talking their way through complicated lives—is akin to discovering a treasure trove. Her characters define themselves through their politics and thinking and are full of foibles she deftly reveals through a satirist's careful eye. She has no meanness of spirit; her approach is curious, not anthropological but absolutely observant. She flinches from nothing.

The very existence of this book feels to me like an assurance that while we may think we have done our archival work and unearthed all the treasures of black thinking women, there is always something more to find. We have literary foremothers who are not just the ones we know we had, who continue to remind us of ourselves: Our minds are intricate. Our desires are complex. We are gorgeously contradictory in our epistemologies. We were not invented yesterday.

Kathleen Collins died too young, so in my searching I also search for traces of the woman herself, one who I feel I know but who I wish I had known. Her voice is so bracing and her eye so clear that I long anew, now that we have found her as a literary voice, for more of how she would have looked at the world: unsparingly but not cynically, analytically, humorously—a black brilliant woman intellectual in a New York state of mind. If I could have only one commentator reading me the human news, I would get everything I need from this one. She represents to me the best of what a New York sensibility can offer: the proxemics of the city, especially in certain neighborhoods and at certain moments in time, means that people are on top of each other, constantly crossing, and that no barrio is completely sealed off from other human beings. This is the curiosity of life and these are the moments of border crossing that Collins mines so exquisitely. She does not strive to simplify nor does she fear the complexity of black female interiority. Her vision is clear.

Now, this is a literary voice that I can never unhear.

—ELIZABETH ALEXANDER

EXTERIORS

"Okay, it's a sixth-floor walk-up, three rooms in the front, bathtub in the kitchen, roaches on the walls, a cubbyhole of a john with a stained-glass window. The light? They've got light up the butt! It's the tallest building on the block, facing nothin' but rooftops and sun. Okay, let's light it for night. I want a spot on that big double bed that takes up most of the room. And a little one on that burlap night table. Okay, now light that worktable with all those notebooks and papers and stuff. Good. And put a spot on those pillows made up to look like a couch. Good. Now let's have a nice soft gel on the young man composing his poems or reading at his worktable. And another soft one for the young woman standing by the stove killing roaches. Okay, now backlight the two of them asleep in the big double bed with that blue-and-white comforter over them. Nice touch.

"Okay, now while they're asleep put a spot on the young woman smiling in that photograph taken on the roof of the building and on the young man smoking a pipe in that photograph taken in the black rocking chair, and be sure to light the two of them hugging each other in that photograph taken in the park around the corner. Good. Now backlight the young woman as she lifts that enamel counter covering the bathtub and put a little light on him undressing her and a nice soft arc on the two of them nude in the doorway. Nice touch. Now dim the light. He's picking at her and teasing her. No, take it way down. She looks too anxious and sad. Keep it down. He looks too restless and angry. Down some more. She's just trying to please him. It can stay down. She's just waiting at the window. No, on second thought, kill it, he won't come in before morning. Okay. Now find a nice low level while they're lying without speaking. No, kill it, there's too much silence and pain. Now fog it slightly when he comes back in the evening and keep it dim while they sit on the bed. Now, how about a nice blue gel when he tells her it's over. Good. Now go for a little fog while she tries not to cry. Good. Now take it up on him a little while he watches her coldly, then up on her when she asks him to stay. Nice. Now down a bit while it settles between them and keep it down while he watches her, just watches her, then fade him to black and leave her in the shadow while she looks for the feelings that lit up the room."

INTERIORS

HUSBAND

. . . It's a long improvisation, my life . . . I don't know
many musicians who could come up with the variations I have . . . like a poet with a third eye for the way
that the wind blows . . . I put my token in the great
subway train and went for a ride. I'm a moody son of a
bitch. When I was a kid I used to hide in my closet and
shit . . . keep the little buggers out of my room. I was
never a pleasure to have around . . . too moody . . .
an intimidating nuisance flyleafing his way across time
on a whim, any old whim . . . appalled by the mirthless
accommodation of adulthood . . . you loved me like a
god and so accommodated yourself instantly to all my
whims . . . fancifying them into significant escapades
of the soul . . . while all along I was igniting myself at

will ... I'm moody, damn it, and restless ... and life has so many tuneless days ... I can't apologize for loving you so little. Only dreams carry the sweet logic I respect ... dreams ... and a certain ... insouciance ... primevally inaccessible to your nature. You were born sincere, well-meaning, without duplicity ... I was born a son of a bitch, an asshole, a self-accommodating sentimentalist slowing down any old chariot in sight ... for a ride. I love everything too little except the journey, the way the wheels turn ... I'm just a passenger on the train of life ... Of all the dreams I've satisfied, perhaps making money was the most ... penetrating ... it permitted me to find out once and for all the real shape of things, how to fit things to size ... it was almost a physical pleasure, replacing the magic potion I used to find in my dick ... it enabled me to take hold of life concretely and measure it ... you always smell nice, lady ... when I moved in with Ramona you had a minor stroke ... you still can't use two of your fingers ... it was a whim, lady, don't you understand that? It was a whim, just an idea, because she was so simpleminded she fascinated me ... but you took it to heart and let it deal you a fatal blow ... no woman living has ever been part of my dreams ... you should have known that ...

the accommodation would be too brutal for so ill-equipped a soul . . . I'm too moody . . . I don't make you happy . . . I never made anybody happy, not any of those women you have spent your life being jealous of . . . you're a funny woman . . . you remember that surprise party you gave me when I turned forty . . . that's still far and away the best party I've ever been to . . . you made this rum punch that you let sit in the freezer for days, and it was so potent people didn't get drunk they got disembodied, so that when Sam began to play all his Cuban music . . . You remember that? . . . He started playing these long-ass Latin records where each song lasted about an hour and everybody was floating so high by that time they got caught inside the beat and couldn't stop dancing . . . it was the weirdest thing I ever saw . . . a disembodied orgy . . . people would look at me with a positive glow in their eyes, like they were inside some kind of bubble, and say . . . "great party, man . . . great fuckin' party" . . . it was a gas . . . the shit I remember . . . I was out at Coney Island one time . . . with Ramona, and we were walking along the beach and suddenly she aborted . . . just like that . . . the baby dropped out of her onto the sand . . . she told me she could do that anytime she got pregnant . . . she just concentrated real hard and she could make her womb give it up . . . she was at the party, you know . . . you'd never seen her . . . it was weird . . . watching her watch you and you not knowing who she was . . . sometimes when I was dancing with her, it seemed to me that your eyes got a funny look, like they sensed something . . . but then you would smile . . . and throw me a birthday kiss . . . you were very beautiful that night . . . Ramona was jealous of you . . . that gave me a weird pleasure and I fell in love with you again . . . I felt toward you exactly like I had when we first lived together . . . it was incredible . . . you were the same person again, and I was the same person again, and you were walking into the apartment with that smile and that glow, heating up the place . . . and I loved you so much again I was crying . . . it was so fucking real, I could smell that sweet smell you had about you when you slept . . . and I would curl up under you just to smell you because it made me feel so peaceful and happy . . . I could *touch* it it was so real . . . and then it was gone, and I was dancing with Ramona at my birthday party . . . and watching you blow me a birthday kiss . . . you have made do with so little . . . sometimes I get the feeling that when I'm dead happiness is gonna rise up out of your soul and wreak havoc on life . . . I won't apologize for loving you so little . . . life has so many tuneless days . . . what better posture to take than to become a whimsical motherfucker? Can you think of a better one? I never could. Be a husband? Or a father? In exchange for being a whimsical motherfucker? You got to be crazy . . . I have to have room to improvise, lady, some way to ignite myself into life. I have to have room to improvise . . . life has so many tuneless days . . .

WIFE

. . . The first time my husband left me, I took a small cabin in the woods . . . to enjoy a benevolent solitude. I brought one suitcase with me, a photograph of myself looking serene and wistful, some drawings to hang on the wall, and my violin . . . I planned to go swimming every day in the stream behind the cabin, take long walks in the woods, and practice my violin. I was going to stay the whole summer. I stayed three days. During those three days I swam in the morning, practiced my violin until the noontime hour, ate lunch, and went for a walk in the woods. The walks left me hot and sweaty, so when I got back to the cabin, I heated water for a sponge bath, then made some tea. On the third day, when I came back from my walk, I was about to heat some water when the kerosene stove caught fire. I took a blanket to the flames, but they had already covered half the room. For a long while I stood there, trying to think of something to do. Then, in a flash, I realized I hadn't a second to waste if I was to leave there alive. So I jumped through a screen, stark naked. Some farmers came along, puzzled by the sight of all this brown flesh against a backdrop of raging flames . . . the fire burned my hair, my clothes, my violin. Nature is beautiful that way . . . she leaves you with nothing to say. . . . I came back home, bought a large flower box for the kitchen window, and began to grow herbs . . . it was very hot and lonely . . . I took a job illustrating children's stories and attended my herbs, planting and digging till my fingers dripped with earth and I had to brush stray hairs out of my eyes . . . streaking my face with sweat and dirt . . . pouring into my planting every image of a budding herbalist devouring her loneliness in sweat and dirt and straying hairs and labeling them *thyme* and *rosemary* and *sage* . . . the basil descended below into a neighbor's window while the rosemary inverted itself and took root in the kitchen . . . the summer grew hotter and lonelier . . . I took to crossing the Brooklyn Bridge in the evenings between six and eight at the time the sun was setting, and in the glow of sunset I relieved the outer edges of my sadness, letting it blend with the surf-like monotony of the cars splashing below and the faint, luminescent splendor of the New York skyline . . . then came a period when nothing soothed me . . . there was no balm in the festive herbal splendor of my kitchen, no balm in the exhaustive evening showers before and after the Brooklyn Bridge excursion . . . the waking hours weighted themselves between my legs, and there was no relief in sight . . . I took to the reading of memoirs . . . it was one of my finer moments when I discovered that no human life escapes the tribulation of solitude . . . to the Claudes and Johns and Marthas and Henrys of past lives I owe my first real penetration of life's lamentations, passed on from father to son and then back again . . . I lay collapsed on a bed of sorrowful immersion and discovery from five thirty Friday evenings until eight thirty Monday mornings . . . other souls had suffered such extremes of separation and abandon, and in their wit and irony and quaint homiletic posturing I momentarily lifted myself out of myself and onto a plane of spiritual lamentation . . . the summer grew hotter and lonelier . . . a friend had a baby and my abandon incarnated itself in this lively, bubbly creature, causing the most extreme anguish I had yet experienced . . . I began to feel that I was drying out inside . . . that cold waves were shriveling my breasts and my limbs began to shriek and sputter . . . at night you surfaced in my sleep: unbuttoning yourself in front of a diverse sampling of salesgirls, waitresses, go-go dancers, and deaconesses . . . I thought I was turning into cardboard . . . you were filling someone else's belly . . . a cold longing weighted itself between my legs . . . the pain dried me out . . . summer was almost over . . . I went to the nearest art supply store and purchased a piece of cardboard, 9" × 12" . . . from an old junk shop I returned with armfuls of ancient magazines . . . I would create a massive collage to decorate the wall opposite my bed. The clutter and disarray created an illusion of warmth, of busy, cozy, fun-loving solitude . . . I snipped and pasted, snipped and pasted . . . pouring into my masterpiece the frenetic, absorbed posture of the woman artist at work . . . it encouraged me to consider a little light fucking . . . so on a frisky Sunday morning I went romping through the Botanic Garden . . . he turned out to be tall, fervently sincere behind thick bifocals . . . and with a penis about the size of a pea . . . I took it as an omen that I was not designed for light fucking . . . it was fall . . . you called long-distance collect . . . I asked you for a baby . . . you laughed and agreed to call me again this time next year . . . the summer came back hotter and lonelier. I met a jazz disc jockey and determined again on a little light fucking . . . he came home with me one night when the snipping and pasting had collaged itself onto the couch, onto the fireplace, onto the rug and the curtains and the bathroom mirror . . . and Duco Cement adhered to your soles upon entry . . . the jazz disc jockey found me . . . surprising . . . but not knowing what else to do he slipped insipidly inside me out of embarrassment and came without the least bit of pleasure. . . . Fall came back for good . . . I began to sew . . . turning out an astonishing assortment of ill-fitting slacks, blouses, velvet dresses, and lounging pajamas . . . pouring into this meticulous work a host of images about the beauty of craftsmanship and the fulfillment of working with one's hands. . . . Winter came . . . I rode the subway to Coney Island. The cold, lonely stretch of beach, the abandoned amusement park figured in a poem entitled "In the Winter of Our

Love" . . . you surfaced again at midnight, while I sat before the fire . . . unbuttoning yourself in front of the woman of your dreams . . . more beautiful, more kind, more loving than me . . . I considered buying another violin . . . the last one got burned alive in a fire, in the woods, at the beginning of summer . . .

THE UNCLE

I had an uncle who cried himself to sleep. Yes, it's quite a true story and it ended badly. That is to say, one night he cried himself to death. He was close to forty. A former athlete of Olympic stature. In my father's house there are still gold trophies received while he was in England for the Olympics of some year. He was quite handsome. Negro. But a real double for Marlon Brando. A story runs through my family that one day, on a street in Philadelphia, my uncle and Marlon Brando passed each other and stopped, each stunned by the resemblance. He was quite fair anyway, a light brown but with the same brooding Brando-esque face, the pouty jowl around the cheeks and mouth, the disappointed eyes moody and restless. He was my favorite uncle. It is difficult to separate this story from the slight props of race necessary to bolster it up. I have said he was Negro. A track star of some standing. A double for Marlon Brando. He had, too, an exquisite wife of such mixed breeding that her skin was the palest white imaginable, hair black and silky, her features keen. As children my sister and I idolized them. To have such a stunning aunt and uncle! And they loved us, too. We spent many summers in the small southern New Jersey town where they lived, in the house that once belonged to my grandmother and now belonged to them. They were always quite broke. I remember once my sister and I turned over the last of our pennies to pay the electric bill while a worker stood in the doorway ready to cut it off. But that only added to their magic in our eyes. To be broke but still so handsome and beautiful, lazy and generous. For my uncle could no longer run because of the severe asthma attacks that had just begun. And already he had the habit of reclining for days at a time on the living room couch and never moving. And my aunt never worked. It seems that I can recall stretches of days when my sister and I would wake up, go into their bedroom, and the four of us would lie there for hours, laughing and hearing stories. My aunt loved to talk about sex. Without her

I still might not know its place in the full scheme of procreation. And my uncle loved to order huge submarine sandwiches, hot chocolate, powdered doughnuts, and ice cream from the luncheonette around the corner and lie in bed eating and talking. When I take the hallowed filter away from those snug summer days I see now that already he had lost the will to struggle with life and that my aunt was a lazy, spoiled woman who thought her fair, almost-white skin would save her. I lost touch with my family early. Went abroad for several years, came back married, and began a family of my own. But my father's letters told of my uncle's slow disintegration, his off-again, on-again jobs as a track coach at various colleges and recreation centers, his long paralytic bouts of depression when he took to his bed for weeks at a time and cried day and night.

I saw him only once during those years: at my parents' summer home, where I came to spend a few weeks after the birth of my first child. He came in the front door as I was coming down the steps. He looked the same to me, except the brooding Brando looks had deepened, the sad pout now creased his forehead and beneath his eyes and made his mouth droop a little more.

But I was fascinated by this deepening, perhaps because I was still young enough to be attracted to sorrow. Then a strange thing happened. In the middle of the night he woke me up, shook me awake with his violent crying and sobbing and begged me to come downstairs and talk with him.

I did.

We sat up the rest of the night, and he cried with only slight coherent moments in between, when he would mumble about my aunt, how she had turned out to be stupid, lazy, no real help to him; how he had never amounted to anything, never been able to count on anyone. How he could cry! Give in to his crying, allow it full possession of his being as if life were a vast well of tears and one must cry to be at the center of it! My father came down, awakened by us, angry and furious at his brother for putting me through such an ordeal.

I never saw him again. But I was having dinner with my parents when the phone call came that told of his death. My father was badly shaken. It was the first of his seven brothers and sisters to die. Yet he was the baby, the last born, the one whom all the others had loved and pampered and spoiled the most. I offered to

drive down with my father to his house. On the way
my father filled me in on the last years of his life, the
years when he never left the bed. How night after night
he kept everyone awake (for somehow in those years
he had managed to produce three now almost-grown
children) with his laments, his great heartrending sobbing that went on hour after relentless hour until the
morning, when he would fall asleep and sleep the day
away only to awaken again at night and begin this vigi-
lant lamentation. His children had grown up inside his
sorrow. His brothers and sisters would come time and
time again and try to coax him back into life, stand
at the bottom of the steps and beg him to come as far
as the living room, bring succulent meals and plead
with him to come down and share them, promise to
find him work as the head track coach at some presti-
gious university. But he kept to his bed, his mournful
inverted existence; cried in his pillow until death took
him away.

My aunt opened the door. With the years she'd kept
all her beauty except around the eyes—the washed-out
eyes of a woman who has put up with too much. The
house was much as I remembered it. The living room
couch where I would watch him stretch out with his

huge submarine sandwiches and powdered doughnuts. The dining room, which now held only near-white women, older variations of my aunt sitting together sipping sherry and whispering. I went upstairs to his bedroom. The wide old-fashioned bed where he'd lived dominated the room, stood there like a monument to his perverse pursuit of humiliation and sorrow. It was surely perverse, surely bound to the color of his skin and its bastard possibilities. But his weeping, wailing, and gnashing of teeth brimmed potent to overflowing in the room, and I began to weep for him, weep tears of pride and joy that he should have so soaked his life in sorrow and gone back to some ancient ritual beyond the blunt humiliation of his skin, with its bound-and-sealed possibilities; so refused to overcome his sorrow as some affliction to be transcended, some stumbling block put in his way for the sake of trial and endurance; so refused to strike out against it, go down in a blaze of responsibilities met and struggled with. No. He utterly honored his sorrow, gave in to it with such deep and boundless weeping that it seemed as I stood there he was the bravest man I had ever known.

HOW DOES ONE SAY

When she left home for the summer her hair was so short her father wouldn't say good-bye. He couldn't bear to look at her. She had it cut so short there wasn't any use straightening it, so it frizzed tight around her head and made her look, in her father's words, "just like any other colored girl."

She was on her way to Maine to summer school to speak nothing but French for six weeks. She drove all the way from New Jersey. Crying. Undermined by the way her father had looked at her. His severe gray eyes hating that his daughter should look so colored, that she should have done away with the one thing that made her different, that she should be going to Maine looking like that when more than likely she would be the only one or almost the only one, and did she have to be the only one or almost the only one and look so colored, look "just like any other colored girl"?

When she went to register for class she kept a scarf on her head and didn't look at anyone (which would have embarrassed her father even more because he had always insisted that she stand erect, look people directly in the eye, and not act sheepish). But she was feeling very insecure and ugly without her hair. And, of course, very colored.

And yet she did notice his eyebrows, and whenever she recalled that first meeting she saw her own brown face with a green-and-white scarf around it and his thick, bushy eyebrows facing her and laughing. The thickest, the bushiest brows!! And the eyes beneath them that kept a cool, steady gaze. They shook hands . . . *"Professeur . . ."* *"Mademoiselle . . ."*

She went back to her room, washed and combed her hair and let it alone. Then she dressed and went to dinner.

He was mixing the salad. *Professeur . . .* with the bushy eyebrows. *"Bonsoir, mademoiselle."* A voice not gay but pleased, with those clear, steady eyes and a laughing frown, almost as if the weight of his eyebrows caused a perpetual frown that made him look solemn

and silly at the same time. *"Et vous, mademoiselle . . .
d'où venez-vous?"*

After supper he was standing on the lawn . . . *en-
tre les professeurs* . . . and he watched her walk by. He
watched. She knew she was being watched. It was like
a wire going back and forth between them.

On Tuesdays and Thursdays at eleven she took
his course in *civilisation française.* On Mondays and
Wednesdays she had a nine o'clock class that coincided
with his arrival on campus. His car would pass by just
as she crossed the lawn . . . it was important to both
of them to be there on time for that crossing. Though
they never smiled or said hello. Just looked. Just ac-
knowledged that they had both made sure they got
there on time.

Then they met by accident one night in the local
bar. *"Bonjour, mademoiselle . . . que vous êtes élégante
ce soir . . . Je peux vous offrir à boire?"* He invited
her for a drink. He talked. She lost contact with her
French; she felt the words shrivel up and go dry on her
tongue. He talked. *"Vous savez que vous avez de très
jolis yeux?"* She tried to translate word for word . . .
You know that you have some very pretty eyes? . . .
too literal . . . Do you know that you have pretty eyes?

He talked. She watched his bushy eyebrows meet and smile and that made her laugh. She blurted out, *"Après cet été je compte aller vivre à Paris!"* The words came out one at a time. After . . . this . . . summer . . . I . . . intend (hope? plan?) . . . to . . . go . . . live . . . in . . . Paris!! And she went on . . . *"Il me plaît beaucoup de passer l'été ici."* It . . . pleases . . . me . . . very . . . much . . . to . . . spend . . . the . . . summer . . . here . . . She was very pleased with herself. He was very pleased with her. They were very pleased with themselves.

They went for a drive. He talked. *"Vous connaissez le Maine, mademoiselle? C'est un très joli pays. Cela fait quarante-cinq ans que j'habite ici . . . Vous n'étiez même pas née quand je suis arrivé ici comme professeur . . ."* She listened, picking out each phrase separately and giving it a literal translation. Do you know the Maine (that made her laugh), miss? It's a very pretty country. That makes forty-five years that I am here. You were not yet even born when I came here as a professor . . . (why then, he's sixty-five at least . . . why then! . . .). She wanted to tell him he had beautiful eyebrows. *"Comment dit-on 'eyebrows' en français?"* She wanted to tell him how thick and bushy and wonderful they were! *"Comment dit-on 'bushy' en français?"*

And to think, she wasn't yet born when he came here. And then she blurts out, *"Qu'ils sont extraordinaires, vos sourcils! Je les adore!"* In the dark and silent car headed toward the ocean, that makes them laugh . . . *Comment dit-on* . . . how does one say. She could be silly if she wanted to and he wouldn't mind. His eyebrows would crease in a thick, furry way and his eyes would settle their steady, clear gaze on her and he would frown his laughing frown. *Comment dit-on* . . . how does one say . . . You have a laughing frown, Monsieur le Professeur, and I have fallen in love with your laughing frown . . . it goes through me like shock waves. In the dark and silent car headed toward the ocean . . . we *should* be still and silent, this is a shocking and unimaginable situation . . . we should be silent . . . and still . . . because this is shocking and unimaginable. He is talking . . . *"Le malheur dans cette région, c'est que les hivers sont trop longs et l'océan trop froid . . ."* It is the unhappiness . . . (too literal) . . . It is the misfortune in this region that the winters are too long and the ocean is too cold . . . She giggles. *"Comme c'est vrai, monsieur,"* she blurts out. *"Vous dites la vérité, monsieur."* She giggles again . . . How true, mister . . . you are telling the truth!! They are alone in the sand.

He is kneeling in front of her. Her fingernails are biting his flesh. He smiles when he shows her the marks. It is their first secret. *"Vous aimez vous baigner, ma petite?"* . . . *"Oui, monsieur, oui, oui, oui . . . j'aime bien me baigner!"* . . . yes, yes . . . I like to bathe myself . . . (too literal) . . . I like myself to bathe . . . (too literal) . . . I like . . . do you like to bathe yourself, my little one?

It is too shocking and unimaginable, my little one. And she will laugh clean through and shake her short, her unimaginably short and shocking, hair at the sky and accept the full exquisite awakening he will give her . . . *"Comment dit-on* . . . how does one say . . . thank you . . ."

ONLY ONCE

He had to slide down the tunnel with enough poise
left over to execute a faultless jump. Or he would find
himself on the third rail.

He looked at her. "Think I can make it?" He
grinned. Like he could open and close life. With his
laughing eyes. Poised. And his golden body. Poised.

She didn't want to watch. Not this time. Nor any of
the other times.

Once they were walking across the Brooklyn Bridge
when all of a sudden he started climbing up the boul-
ders. The next thing she knew he was walking along
the top. Then she heard herself say to herself, "It's none
of your business, keep walking." And she did.

"It's a gas from up here, baby," he yelled, "even if I
fall it's a fucking gas!"

Only once do you know that kind of man, they say. Only once.

He was leaning against a pole at a dance smoking a Lucky Strike and they started talking. He thought she was funny looking. "You know, you look ridiculous at a dance," he said. "Whatever gave you the idea you belonged at *a dance*?" He took her by the arm and they went across to the park.

"Think you can jump that rock?" He grinned.

She just looked at him.

"Come on, I'll catch you if it looks like you're jumping wrong."

She climbed to the top. Jumped. He watched her and let her fall. She landed okay though her ankle felt a little sore.

"That was beautiful." He grinned. "You could have smashed your ankle to bits."

She felt incredibly proud.

"Let's find another one. I'll catch you if it looks like you're jumping wrong," he said, and hugged her.

Only once do you know that kind of man, they say. Only once.

He rode home with her to New Jersey and she took him into the backyard to look at her father's roses . . .

to look at her childhood, to look at what pricked and stung and was difficult to forgive. He looked at the house and the yard and her family . . . And it seemed to her that everything changed. Was forgiven.

The second time he'd caught her, a fraction of a second before she smashed her ankle. "You almost didn't make it. You jumped wrong." He grinned. Pleased as hell at the split-second way he'd caught her. Pleased as hell.

"Jesus Christ, it's so fucking sweet!" he shouted. And when she turned she could hardly see him for the wisteria, the thin lilac petals crisscrossing his face. "Jesus Christ, what an incredible smell," she shouted. While the perfume slipped under his pores, astounding him, causing a violence to shake him. "Jesus Christ," he shouted, ecstatic with pleasure.

"Think I can make it?" He grinned. Like he could open and close life. With his laughing eyes. Poised. And his golden body. Poised.

Only once do you know that kind of man, they say. Only once.

When she went away he wrote her letters. Thick envelopes would come in the mail. One word to a page. Do. You. Know. How. Much. I. Love. You.

A single rose when they met at the bus stop. And a shit-eating grin on his golden face. Only once, they say. Only once.

They sneaked past his landlady and up to his attic room. It was almost morning. He opened her wide and the dawn came in. She bled like a puppy. Sunlight dazzled them awake. A thick warm grin cuddled her cheek.

Once in the snow on an old fur coat. Once in the woods on a bed of pines. Once in a barn on a pile of hay. Once. Only once.

Now he sits in an armchair with a lamp beside him, and she watches him out of the corner of her eye, while she chatters away with his folks. Now he catches her with a smile that confuses her and makes her trip over her words to meet his eyes . . . "Think I can make it?" He grinned. Like he could open and close life. Bend and twist it.

Now they are in a liquor store on the Bowery. They will buy a giant bottle of Chianti with a long ostrich neck with which they will walk home to 135th Street, drinking huge awkward gulps as they go along. Turning cartwheels and somersaults and landing lopsided in the street. Giggling.

They will be so drunk when they get home that they will collide together on the floor and everything will blur. Then thin secrets will trickle out, about how once he was surprised by life, deeply surprised, when his golden skin turned black and called forth contempt, when the laughter in his eyes died. Later she will try to pinpoint the exact secret reaching her in the fog. Later she will try to pinpoint when laughter died. Later she will try to pinpoint who threw the insult and when and where it landed and why it stuck to his skin. But she will not be able to. It will thin out by morning. Dilute to a tiny scab that will not fall off.

"Think I can make it?" He grinned. Like he could open and close life. With his laughing eyes. Poised. And his golden body. Poised.

He didn't clear the rail. Or maybe he did. Maybe it was later. He mistimed a dive from a high cliff. Or maybe he didn't. Maybe it was even later than that. He shot himself in the head. Thought the gun was empty. Or maybe he knew it wasn't.

Only once do you know that kind of man, they say. Only once. But she would know them all her life. One after the other they would turn out to be that kind of man.

WHATEVER HAPPENED TO INTERRACIAL LOVE?

An apartment on the Upper West Side shared by two interracial roommates. It's the year of "the human being." The year of race-creed-color blindness. It's 1963. One roommate ("white") is a Harlem community organizer, working out of a storefront on Lenox Avenue. She is twenty-two and fresh out of Sarah Lawrence. She is twenty-two and in love with a young Umbra poet (among whom in later life such great names as Imamu Baraka and Ishmael Reed will be counted the most illustrious members). The other roommate ("negro") has just surfaced from the jail cells of Albany, Georgia. She is twenty-one and the only "negro" in her graduating class. She is in love with a young, defiant freedom rider ("white") who has just had his jaw dislocated in a Mississippi jail. He is sitting with her at the breakfast table, his mouth wired for sound.

Among those who pass in and out of this inter-racial mecca: a photographer ("negro") who in a desperate moment just rifled their typewriter and headed toward the nearest pawn shop; a young, vital heroin addict ("negro") off the streets of Harlem whose constant companion is another nubile Sarah Lawrence girl ("white"); the Umbra poet ("negro"), who is drinking coffee in the front room and reading a verse called "June Bug!"; an assortment of bright-eyed women ("white") fresh from a prayer vigil on the steps of our nation's Capitol; a few rebellious-looking women ("negro") en route to Itta Bena, Mississippi, to renounce their northern bourgeois heritage. Idealism came back in style. People got along for a while. Inside the melting pot. Inside the melting pot.

It's summer. The "negro" roommate and her young white lover are considering marriage. In a while, she'll take him to the hospital to meet her father (a stroke victim from an overdose of idealism). In a while, her short white lover with the overhung lip (so that he stuttered slightly) will confront the gray-haired distinction of New Jersey's first "colored" principal. (". . . I love you," he said . . . her lover, that is . . . "I want to be a Negro for you," he said . . .) Her father will fix his deep gray bourgeois eyes on her and not move a muscle.

It's summer. The Sarah Lawrence graduate is listening to her Umbra poet. He is dark and quiet, and his eyes dart back and forth across her face while he reads. The apartment is growing dusky (*and* dusty). Later the coterie will prepare to attend a rent strike meeting in Harlem, or a fundraising benefit for SNCC, or a voter registration meeting in Newark, New Jersey.

We are in the year of racial, religious, and ethnic mildew. "Negro" families in Montclair, New Jersey; Brookfield, Massachusetts; Hartford, Connecticut; Mount Vernon, New York; Washington, D.C.—the hidden enclaves of the *Black Bourgeoisie* (a book that will be taken down from the dusty shelves of some obscure small-town library and soon issued in paperback, causing the fortunes of an obscure "negro" sociologist to rise—will see their children abandon a lifetime of de-ghettoizing. Their sons will go to jail for freedom (which in their parents' minds is no different from going to jail for armed robbery, heroin addiction, pimping, and other assorted ethnic hustles).

Their daughters will kneel in prayer on the dusty red-clay roads of Georgia, as if the neat, velvet pews of the Episcopal Church had never been their first encounter with religion. The "First Coloreds" in medicine, law, politics, baseball, education, engineering, basketball, biochemical research, the armed services, tennis, and film production will all be asked to come forward and speak about their success. Ralph Bunche will become a household name. Everyone who is anyone will find at least one "negro" to bring along home for dinner. It's the year of the human being. It's 1963: Whatever happened to interracial love?

In our Upper West Side apartment our young ("negro") roommate has just come back from the hospital with her freedom rider. She is ashamed and strangely depressed. The bleak look in her father's eyes was not reassuring. He could not move a muscle, yet he seemed to be saying, Is it for *this* that I fought and struggled all these years, for *this, this,* indecent commingling? He does not seem to understand the shape of the world to come. He does not seem to understand that this young colored woman he has spawned does not, herself, believe in color: that to her the young freedom rider of her dreams is colorless (as indeed he is), that their feel-ings begin where color ends (as indeed they must), that if only he could understand that race as an issue, race as a social factor, race as a political or economic stum-bling block—race is part of the past. Can't he see that love is color-free? She is close to tears. The gray bour-geois eyes remain fixed in her mind.

Her lover sits dejectedly in the sunless room. (When they took the apartment, she chose the back bedroom just off the foyer, thinking it would provide her greater privacy. It does, but it is also without light, and by the end of her time there she will discover that almost all her unhappiness stemmed from that dark and dusky corridor she called her room. It was only sunlight she needed. Pure, delicious sunlight flooding through a room.) He is thinking about his parents, about his stern Bostonian upbringing. His father will not even venture to meet the girl he has chosen to marry. His mother will agree only to a secret rendez-vous in some out-of-the-way Boston restaurant. How can he bring his father to an understanding of what it feels like to be beaten to a pulp? Teeth mashed in, jaw dislocated, nose rearranged, stomach pulpy. And all for freedom. All for the "negroes" of this land we call

America. It is imperative that his father understand that he has not been betrayed, that he, the son, is in fact trying to fulfill the father's dream—that dream that he, the father, believes in deep, deep down. Somewhere way deep down. He, the son. It's 1963: we're in the year of prophetic fulfillment. The last revival meeting is at hand, where the sons took up the cross of the fathers. White sons went forth to the dirt roads of Georgia and Alabama to prove to their fathers that the melting pot could still melt. "Negro" sons went forth to the Woolworths and Grants and Greyhounds of America to prove to their fathers that they could eat and sit and ride as well in the front as in the back, as well seated as standing.

Her lover sits in the sunless room feeling dejected. Soon he is to return to the cotton fields for some more "grassroots organizing." His Boston accent flirts with the edges of a Southern drawl. His white face floats in a sea of black protest. It is a time that calls forth the most picturesque of metaphors, for we are swimming along in the mythical underbelly of America . . . there where it is soft and prickly, where you may rub your nose against the grainy sands of illusion and come up bleeding.

Our young lover ("white"), upon his return, will land in jail a second time, where he will refuse to post bail, refuse to eat, refuse to keep his mouth shut until he is again beaten into irrational silence, his mouth once more wired for sound. His father does not come to his aid. His mother begs him to use the enclosed check and come home. His ("negro") lady writes him poetic letters from her Upper West Side apartment with here and there a little Emily Dickinson for encouragement ("Who are you? / I'm Nobody!") and a little Edna St. Vincent Millay when a more elegiac mood reigns ("If I should learn, in some quite casual way, / That you were gone, not to return again"). They will pass the winter in this desultory fashion.

The ("negro") roommate takes refuge in her sunless room. In the face of her father's paralytic sternness, in the face of her lover's imprisonment, she sits, sips tea, and relives the "negro" void of her college years (what was it like to be *the only one*????).

She recalls her father's freshman admonition on how to avoid the roommate problem (EEEEK!!!! There's a "negro" in my room!!!): always request a single. She remembers each one of those singles—one for every year. Though she was never lonely. They made her class president (for freshman openers), then honor board representative (for sophomore encores), then class something-or-other the year after that . . . she was sure she was one of them, until that fateful day THE SIT-INS STARTED, and she began to wonder why, in fact, she was so privileged when, according to THE SIT-INNERS (who came in droves to lecture at every near-white institution in the country), many of the members of her race (they were still a long way away from being "her people") were living in poverty and despair, deprived even of the right to vote, a basic American right. Yet they were Americans, just as she herself was an American. So at Easter time she announced to her father (who had not yet had his stroke) that she would be going south that summer to work as a voter registration worker, that she would be going south that summer to find out once and for all what it was like to be a "negro."

And that summer had brought her one startling and overwhelming realization, that she could marry *anyone,* not just a colored doctor/dentist/lawyer/educator, but *anyone:* A Mexican truck driver. A Japanese psychiatrist. A South African journalist. Anyone. Up to and including a white man. This was the ripest fruit from a summer spent picking cotton and cucumbers, and taking sunbaths in Momma Dolly's chicken yard with another "negro" friend who was also escaping her bourgeois past. They were turning themselves into earth women, black (the word surfaces!) women of the soil, in harmony with the ebb and flow of nature, in harmony with the Southern earth of their ancestry, and the deep Southern sky, and the moody Southern stars.

It was there that she met her young lover ("white"), who shared their bare existence of corn bread and chitterlings, while together they combed the hot dirt roads pleading with folks to come out and vote, come out and be shot, come out and lay down their life on the interracial line. She had an ear for public speaking. She attributed this to some Southern ancestry deeply ignored by her parents (and never let it occur to her that her father before his paralytic crisis was himself a most persuasive speaker). She loved standing in the pulpit with outstretched arms, tears rolling down her cheeks, offering herself to freedom and begging others to join her, join this great hand-holding, we-shall-overcome bandwagon of interraciality when black and white would, in fact, walk hand-in-hand to freedom.

A shiver curved down her spine. She sat still in the sunless room and remembered. The fear. That she had pushed somewhere out of reach. That she had refused to acknowledge, until the day they shot holes all through Momma Dolly's farm and she came home. To her last year of school. To make speeches, and sing songs, and raise money. But never, ever to go back. Not even when the leader of the movement himself begged her to use her college degree and come back and teach. She would make speeches and sing and raise money and send clothes. But never go back. Except through the eyes of her lover ("white"), who lay awake nights in that same Mississippi jail. That was the closest she ever came to a return.

She closes her eyes for a moment. She is reading *The Rise and Fall of the Third Reich; Toward a Psychology of Being; Rabbit, Run; The Centaur* ("Listen to me, lady. I love you, I want to be a Negro for you . . ."). And every Wednesday at five o'clock she sat for an hour and unburdened herself on a very sleepy psychiatrist, whose continual dozing was a sure sign that not only was *she* boring, but that any life dissected too closely was boring and could only make you fall asleep. He diagnosed her as manic-depressive. All negroes were prone to manic depression, he told her. They were all subject to frenzied highs, followed by sudden, depressive lows, he told her. It must have to do with all that singing and dancing, he told her. So she went to the library and looked up manic-depressive, to catalog her symptoms and hang them on her wall: prone to ecstatic moments followed by severe depressions with accompanying loss of self-esteem, feelings of meaninglessness, and a sense of the insignificance of life (later she would laugh when she discovered that meaninglessness came from the dark shaft of gloom that surrounded her day and night, and that ecstasy was just a sunny room away).

She wished her father would forgive her lapses. Her racial ones as well as her sexual ones. After her first night in bed, she was astonished: *That* was what the fuss was all about? *That* was why her father watched over her with lock and key, scrutinizing every date as a potential enemy? For *that*?? That peculiar slipping and sliding that occasionally provided a momentary gasp. A strange, slight convulsion. And then what? How could her father think she was going to the dogs because she had slept with one man and was about to marry another one ("white," true)? And what of it? She wished her father could talk, that he didn't just lie there and stare at her like she was really "colored," like now she had really turned into "a colored woman" and was beyond salvation. That was the real bug. Not that she had "opened the doors to herself," as her mother put it, but that she had ceased to be her father's adored child. She had even committed the final sin, the unforgivable final sin of ("negro") girlhood: she had cut her hair. "How few negro girls are blessed with long hair?" her father had sobbed. "How could you go and turn yourself into a negro just like any other negro? How could you do that?" And he turned and walked away. She could feel her skin turning darker while he lay there and stared at her; her hair felt not only short but unbelievably bushy. At any moment a toothless grin would spread across her face and she would be a walking replica of all of his nightmares— she would shuffle backward and grin and her bushy hair would stand on end and she would have turned into "a colored woman." That was what she read in those gray bourgeois eyes; that was what caused the stroke: the sudden transformation of his beloved, intelligent daughter (she *was* the only "negro" to graduate from that alpine fortress) into "a colored woman." Such thoughts left her sticky and glued to her seat. If only she could abolish the gloom and let herself blossom under the light of this interracial love affair. If nothing else they would have beautiful children. They always were, these interracial urchins produced out of Chinese and white fusion, or Indian and negro fusion, or, for that matter, white and negro fusion; as if through the process of mating the children took the best of all the features: added a little kink to the too-straight white hair, chiseled into aquiline the too-broad negro nose, rounded the tight, slinky Chinese eyes to a delicate almond shape. She liked thinking about a little interracial baby of her own. She put her hand on her stomach and opened her eyes. The room was dark. Even with two 150-watt bulbs, the room was dark. She heard her roommate open the door.

Her roommate was a healthy-looking girl (whose name was Charlotte, by the way): the kind of girl who adored a lovable sheepdog at the age of three, and rode horses bareback at five; the kind of girl who was bred, not raised. And it showed, particularly around the eyes, and in the deep healthy glow of the skin. It showed. With a trace of interracial rebellion in every strand of that vibrant blond hair.

If her roommate was healthy looking, she, by comparison, was a bit anemic looking. She was, for instance, too pale for a "negro" with something a bit too yellow around the gills. Four years in the north woods of academia had given her very little opportunity to dress chicly as ("negro") women notoriously do, with a flair for the right place to hang a scarf, cock a hat, don a cacophony of colors with an uncanny, unerring taste for making it work. She had no such flair. Had, in fact, no flair whatsoever. If you thought of any color at all beside her, it was brown. That monotonous brown that goes well with a pair of Buster Brown shoes. Her first lover ("negro") had attempted some improvements on her looks. He had suggested, for example, that she eliminate that brushstroke of bright orange smeared inaccurately across her lips, that she stop those clumsy efforts at tweezing her thick, bushy eyebrows that were, in fact, her best feature. Suggested, in sum, that she stop trying to do something with herself, but instead just wear turtleneck sweaters (preferably black ones to go with her Buster Brown shoes) and one plain corduroy skirt with big pockets. Which she did. Even after they broke up (he took a motorcycle and headed out west with a new ["white"] girlfriend).

Her roommate is reminding her that there is a poetry reading tonight down at St. Mark's in-the-Bowery and would she like to go with them? It's an Umbra reading. She's trying to decide when the key turns again in the lock and Henry ("negro"), the poet, enters. They are actually living *à trois* and sometimes *à quatre* when what's-his-face takes a brief furlough from jail. Right now there are only three of them. Henry is unquestionably endearing. With the softest voice you ever heard. Charlotte (her roommate) is considering supporting him for life. He could write poetry, she could work. It is not a particularly political dream—Henry is not about to go south and sit in, he is not even interested in voter registration, and his poems are curiously apolitical. It is really a romance, which will eventually pop (if one is willing to admit that romances are a bit like balloons). Charlotte found she didn't like working. Even for poetry. Henry read about her wedding in the *New York Times* (Sunday section). But we are light-years away from this eventual outcome.

It's 1963. The windows to this ground-floor interracial mecca are always wide open. An assortment of people avoid the door and come in through the windows. There's Adrienne ("white"), another long-haired beauty of the Sarah Lawrence variety. She spends all her time with Skip, the ghetto youth with the heroin problem. She and Charlotte spend hours trying to devise ways to help Skip kick the habit and become a full-time rent strike organizer with the other part of his time taken up with solving his daily problem. They see him as a beautiful human being "caught in the currents of a segregated existence"; they fervently believe that their own infiltration of his lifestyle, their own willingness to live among him (and *with* him, if the need arises), will surely change all this. Integration is a pulsating new beat, which will liberate him from the old, segregated ways of doing things. For is it not, after all, *we* who must overcome? WE, who must walk hand-in-hand? For if you (Skip) are not free, then it follows, as night follows day (an exquisite metaphor for our purpose), that I (Adrienne) am not free. Togetherness came back in style. People got along for a while. Inside the melting pot.

There is a tall, somber young man (West Indian, and West Indians are not "negroes") called Derek, who always rings the bell and waits politely to be admitted. He sits in the corner of Charlotte's room (all the congregating takes place in Charlotte's room, which faces the street and the light and the . . . we could go on) and pontificates. In his methodical, messianic mind there is a theory building that perhaps integration is just another form of imitation, that perhaps integration is just another form of stultification, that perhaps integration is just another form of impersonation, that perhaps . . . and a year later he will shout from the podium, "Black Power! Black Power! Black Power!" and the romance will go up in smoke (if one is willing to admit that romances are a bit like smoldering fires).

There is another quiet, diligent soul who frequents this integrated coterie. A prophetic soul who is looked upon as the Father of the Movement. He comes only to persuade everyone that they should use their education in the service of the massive voter education program he is starting in Mississippi. Its aim: to increase the literacy rate of Southerners ("negroes") and prepare them for political activity. He calls it the politics of arithmetic. He has understood that politics is the source of power and that Southern arithmetic (ten negroes + one white = eleven whites) should be reversed. It is a stunningly correct analysis that will go down in defeat at the Democratic Convention of 1964, when that illustrious body turns its back on the New Math. The sands of illusion are prickly and wet, and our prophet will seek a final answer in the Fatherland, as all true prophets must. There is no honor in one's own apartment.

And what of love, instead of politics? What of that nubile, fleeting sensation, when one is color-blind, religion-blind, name-, age-, aid-, vital statistics–blind? What about the love of two "human beings," who mate in spite of or because of or instead of or after the fact of? What of Henry and Charlotte and their possibilities for an integrated cast of children? What of all those interracial couples peppering the Lower East Side in the summer of '63 and the summer of '64, only to go into furtive decline in the summer of '65—no longer to be seen holding hands in public ("Black Power! Black Power! Black Power!")?

But it's 1963 and Cheryl (we have neglected to name her) declines tonight's Umbra festivities. She is tired from reading *The Rise and Fall of the Third Reich;*

Toward a Psychology of Being; Rabbit, Run; and *The Centaur* ("Listen to me, lady. I love you, I want to be a Negro for you . . ."). She will not go with Charlotte and Henry, even though Henry is reading "June Bug!," her favorite poem. She will stay home and practice her stream-of-consciousness therapy, isolating herself in her closet (the only place in her room where her desk fits) and writing automatically, putting down everything that comes into her head (. . . my father sat me down on his lap when Mrs. Drexel slapped me and he told me not to worry about that old librarian slapping me just because I asked if we could take a break and she looked at me like I was a troublemaker and slapped me across the face and the shoe man gave me a pair of tasteless shoes and the brightest red lipstick he had and I insisted loudly that the shoes were in bad taste and the lipstick was too gaudy because I didn't wear shoes like that just because I was colored and couldn't he tell I didn't give off any odor of any kind just because I was colored and that I always held my breath every time I went into his store because I was colored and didn't want to give off any odor of any kind so I tightened my stomach muscles and stopped breathing and that way I knew that nothing unpleasant would escape—not a thought nor an odor nor an ungrammatical sentence nor bad posture nor halitosis nor pimples because I was sucking in my stomach and holding it while I tried on his shoes and couldn't he see that I was one of those colored people who had taste). The book said that if you did this every night for an hour, you could speed up the analytical process, and maybe cure your own self, and Cheryl was very anxious to be cured of her manic depression at a cheaper rate than twenty-five bucks an hour, so she sat in the deep gloom of her room and wrote and wrote and refused to think or punctuate or let her mind do anything but record every single syllable that popped into her head. Censored thoughts were passing out of her unconscious at an amazing rate. Afterward she couldn't lift her wrist from the desk or decipher one syllable. But she was sure she was making progress.

This was always the last performance of the night. Before bedtime. Then she turned out the light and let her thoughts take her to that Mississippi jail cell. Where Alan (as he was prosaically named) rotted. She would compare their sexual coupling ("black" and "white" together) with her first encounter. Did he (Alan) seem smaller simply because she was trying to overcome three hundred years of mythological white impotence in order to mate healthily with him? Or was he smaller? It was a difficult thing to determine. If he *was* smaller, then surely race played no part in it. It was just coincidence that Aaron (the first time they made love it was on the Staten Island Ferry)—

We were very tired, we were very merry—
We had gone back and forth all night on the
    ferry.

—was bigger. Race was not a factor. Sexual fulfillment was color-blind. And she tried to put herself to sleep but couldn't. She began thinking about Charlotte, whom she admired a great deal. There was something incredibly attractive about her healthy, bold looks. She would have liked to have Charlotte's boldness. Her face had a frankness that held your attention.

They had met at a civil rights conference at Sarah Lawrence a year before Charlotte's graduation. Charlotte had come to New York City first (Cheryl didn't graduate until the following year), but whenever Cheryl came to New York for the weekend, she stayed at Charlotte's apartment. They agreed to take an apartment together after Cheryl's graduation. Charlotte was sexually ripe. Beside her Cheryl felt like a novice. It wasn't that they ever talked about sex. They didn't. They talked about babies a lot, though, about what beautiful babies she and Henry would have if they had babies. Charlotte's eyes would look almost dazed with pleasure. But Cheryl was always vaguely irritated by Charlotte and Henry's relationship. In her eyes Henry was too meek. Perhaps because she liked noisy, more vociferous men. Perhaps not. Perhaps Henry was just meek. But his meekness irritated her. She found it subservient. And she disliked him for it. He never got angry, never raised his voice above a whisper, spent all his time in Charlotte's room writing while Charlotte spent all her time in Harlem in a storefront office organizing rent strikes. That didn't seem right.

Once, Cheryl's mother and father came to dinner and Henry was there, too. They all ate in the kitchen at the small round table, and her father's eyes kept filling up with tears. He could not reconcile his daughter to this place. He could not reconcile his daughter to Charlotte (with all her frank breeding spilling all over the place), not to Charlotte and Henry (with all their frank sexuality spilling all over the place). When Cheryl accompanied them to their car, he was still crying. He asked her to come home; he realized now that he had made a terrible mistake sending her to that exclusive school to be the first and only one. It had made her queer. It had made her want a queer life among queer, unnatural people. It was not what he had in mind at all. He had simply wanted her to have a good education with a solid, respected ("white") name behind it. That was all he had wanted. Then he had expected her to come home again and teach and get married and live in the apartment on their third floor. He did not want her to lead this queer integrated life with some pasty freedom rider who liked to flagellate himself for ("negroes"). It was unhealthy. It was wrong. He should go home, too. They should all go home. Henry should go back to his ghetto. Charlotte should return to her well-bred country life. She, Cheryl, should come home and get a job teaching school. Everything else was too queer, too unspeakably queer, and made him cry.

It was not a successful dinner party. Cheryl felt depressed and hid in her closet to try a little automatic writing (Daddy you must see that I must lead my own life even if you don't understand it and all this talk about color all the time I'm not the same anymore and I have to be what I am I've lived with all kinds of people even if they were all white and now I'm trying to live with some white people and some "negro" people and find out who I am and I have to do it and . . .). And then the doorbell rang. Strange. It was past midnight. And she was alone. Henry and Charlotte were still down at another Umbra reading. She peeked cautiously through the keyhole. It was Alan. Out of jail. Standing in the doorway. And crying. No, no, don't touch. He said, No, please. He had something to say: He had just come from his parents' house. He knew now that he could not marry her. He knew now that he would never go back south. It was over. He had come to say good-bye. It was all over. He understood now that he could never be "a negro." Never. Ever. And then he was gone.

She went into her room and sat down. She opened *The Rise and Fall of the Third Reich.* But she couldn't see. Then opened *The Centaur:* "Listen to me, lady. I love you, I want to be a Negro for you . . . But I cannot, quite. I cannot quite make that scene. A final membrane restrains me. I am my father's son . . ." She had never read the ending. She did not know that was how it ended. She had thought it was possible to rupture every membrane and begin at zero.

Then she thought, I must find an apartment high up, around the twentieth floor, where the sun will come flooding in in the morning and I won't awaken inside a deep shaft of gloom. Then I will be able to think and see clearly, about how integration came into style. And people getting along for a while. Inside the melting pot. Inside the melting pot.

It's 1963. Whatever happened to interracial love?

CONFERENCE:
PARTS I AND II

THE RIGHT PERSON (CONFERENCE: PART I)

"Charlie Jones?"

"Yes, ma'am?"

"You're a freedom rider?"

"Yes, ma'am . . ."

"They beat you up in Selma?"

"Yes, ma'am . . ."

"They beat *you* up? With your light skin and your green eyes? How could they do that? Weren't you afraid?"

"The South must be a terrible place. Did you hold hands and pray?"

"Yes, ma'am . . ."

"And they still beat you up?"

"Yes, ma'am . . ."

"You remember how we met? My school sent me to one of those student conferences. You remember? I didn't know anything about civil rights. I came from New Jersey. You sat across from me during a plenary session. You remember? You wanted the conference to take a strong stand on civil rights . . . I kept looking at your freckles and your very light skin, then I heard you say, 'What's your name, young lady?'

"'Mildred Pierce,' I said. 'Miss Pierce,' you said. 'Very nice to meet you, Miss Pierce. I'm Charles Jones, from Johnson C. Smith University.'

"I was suspicious of your shrewd southern voice, the way you looked at me with your washed-out green eyes, the way you sat there smoking Salem cigarettes; all of it intimidated me, you remember?"

"Yes, ma'am . . ."

"You're with the freedom riders?" I said.

"Indeed I am, young lady. Indeed I am . . . And where do you go to school, Miss Pierce?"

"Skidmore College," I said. "I'm president of the freshman class, that's why I got sent to the conference."

"How so, how so . . ." and you lit a Salem. "That's a pretty exclusive school, Miss Pierce."

"I know," I said, "and I'm the first Negro to go there."

"How so, how so . . ."

"And there isn't any prejudice, I just love it."

"How so, how so . . ."

"Do you sit in at lunch counters?" I asked.

"Indeed I do, young lady. Indeed I do." You coughed, choking a bit on your cigarette.

"That must be very discouraging," I said. "It must feel nice to be up north for a change."

"Charlie Jones."

"Yes, ma'am . . ."

"Charlie Jones. I was so excited when you came to see me at school. The girls said, 'He has freckles, Mildred, and green eyes, and he's so good-looking! Are you sure he's a Negro?' I told them that you were, that you'd gotten beat up and even been to jail just for being a Negro. They were really impressed."

"So how's Miss Pierce these days?" you asked.

"Fine," I answered.

"I've been thinking about you a lot since the conference," you said.

"Oh . . ." I said. "How so . . ."

"How so, indeed . . ." You chuckled. "So this is where you go to school, up here inside the rarefied strata of society. It must get kinda lonely."

"Oh no," I said, "I love it! The girls are wonderful!"

"I'll have to take you south, young lady, and open your eyes."

"All right," I said. Eagerly. So eagerly. So eager to please. So thrilled to have a real-life Negro coming into my rarefied atmosphere with real green eyes and freckles and extra-light skin . . . Romance. Romance. Real romance.

"Charlie Jones."

"Yes, ma'am . . ."

"Charlie Jones. I took you home to meet my folks. They set the dining room table for your visit and watched your manners. So eager. So eager. To have a real-life Negro for their daughter. They even forgave your freedom riding. Anything . . . to have a real-life Negro for their daughter."

ひ ひ

"Charlie Jones."

"Yes, ma'am . . ."

"Charlie Jones. The girls at school loved you ('He's so good-looking, he doesn't even look like a Negro!'). My parents found you charming ('Handsome boy,' said my father, 'looks just like one of the family'). That's why I tried it, isn't it?"

"Yes, ma'am . . ."

"Just like that . . . one night I said, 'Take me back to your room, I'll try it with you. It's time for me to try it and you must be the right person.'

"Charlie Jones."

"Yes, ma'am . . ."

"It doesn't seem to go in," you said.

"But it has to," I said, "I know you're the right person . . ."

"Try to relax a little," you said.

"Okay," I said. So eager to please. So thrilled to have a real-life Negro coming into my rarefied atmosphere with real green eyes and freckles and extra-light skin.

"I can't seem to get it in." You chuckled.

"Push with all your might. I'll just relax. I'm sure I can relax. Push and I'll bump. It has to fit. You're the right person. Push hard. You're the right person, I know you are."

"Charlie Jones."
    "Yes, ma'am . . ."
    "It won't go in . . ."
    "No, ma'am . . ."
    "Not even with your green eyes . . ."
    "No, ma'am . . ."
    "And your extra-light skin . . ."
    "No, ma'am . . ."
    "And your freedom riding . . ."
    "No, ma'am . . ."
    "It won't go in . . ."
    "No, ma'am . . ."
    "I guess you're not the right person . . ."

JASON (CONFERENCE: PART II)

I can't get hold of that summer, Jason. It was too lonely. I came home for the last time; from then on I would look for any excuse to keep me away in the summer. But that summer was right after my freshman year and it seemed natural to go home. I took a job at the Lightolier Lamp Company in the complaint department. That was the best thing about the summer. My supervisor was a cross-eyed Jewish lady named Judy, who commiserated loudly with the customers: "What? You didn't get your lamps and they were ordered ten months ago?! Don't you worry about a thing, honey. I'll straighten it out for you . . ." "What? Your three-way floor-to-ceiling light fixture arrived damaged? Take it easy, honey, just leave it to me. You'll have a new one tomorrow . . ." She'd hang up the phone, wink at me, and say, "Honey, see what you can do for those poor people, I gotta get some coffee." Her desk was a confusion of complaints about damaged lamps, lost orders, undelivered merchandise, incorrect shipments, incomplete deliveries . . . I tried to get her to tell me who to call, what forms to fill out, what department to notify . . . "Just let me get my coffee, honey, and I'll tell you everything you need to know . . ." I enjoyed that job. I liked talking to all those people on the phone and sounding efficient and concerned and reassuring . . . "I'm sure I can straighten this out for you, miss . . ." appalled and amused at the fact that there was almost no possibility that I could straighten it out. Then I went home. To eat dinner. To sit on the porch and read to my father, who was anxious and sad that I had no friends. I think I read Dostoyevsky's *Crime and Punishment* all summer long. I see myself carrying it to work and reading it on my lunch hour. I see myself sitting on the porch reading it in the evening while my father seemed to pace back and forth watching me, asking me over and over if I was unhappy. No, I'd say, and smile, and try to concentrate on Raskolnikov. The only excitement I had to look forward to was the National Student Conference in Minneapolis. My school was sending me as a delegate. But that wasn't until the end of August . . . My first plane trip. They boarded us quickly, but then there was some delay and we sat in the plane the longest time before it finally took off. I could see my father on the deck. He waited and waited. He couldn't see me. I waved and waved, and every now and then out of the blue he'd start waving. But he couldn't see me. I was crying. I wish I could remember where I first ran into you . . . I think my father mentioned you would be there while I was packing, but I hadn't planned to look you up. I can't remember where I ran into you. I think it was the cafeteria, but maybe that's because we met there a lot later on . . . I know I felt too brown beside your tiny, almost-albino looks. I know that almost right away I realized you were kind. But your eyes have receded now behind the thick glasses you wear. I don't know why you liked me. I had no taste in clothes (still don't). It was hot and my hair went back quickly. And I already had the beginnings of an ugly fuzz around my chin that bothered me for years. I remember one dress, a checkered tan-and-white sundress with a matching sweater. It was too long. I had it on when you took me to the fair and I know I was wearing it the night I danced for you. The night I danced for you. Why am I recalling such a simple time? We were taking a walk and suddenly I started dancing. I don't know why; it wasn't like me at all. I just wanted to jump outside my colored looks and make you laugh . . . Why am I recalling such a simple time? We said good-bye. We never saw each other again. Once my father mentioned that you'd moved to Washington, become a doctor, married. But all that seemed beside the point. It took so well between us . . .

THE HAPPY FAMILY

"But she came from such a happy family . . ." my friend remarked, ". . . I don't understand how her life got so twisted when she came from such a happy family . . ." And I had to confess my own difficulties in coming to grips with this question. It brought back with such sharpness a strange period in my life when I lived among what I can only describe as a truly happy family. Their whole story passed before my eyes again. I hesitate to tell the tale, it follows such an odd path in my mind. But I have always been fascinated by the idea of a happy family, that remarkable collision of personalities: father, mother, offspring who sometimes fortuitously click; that collision that creates an awe-inspiring environment for the young to radiate, grow, test themselves against a solid, loving rod that does not disappoint. To be so nurtured; to know day after day only comfort, love; to feel your home a happy place where joy and justice meet—this has always seemed to me the greatest gift imaginable. My own nostalgia for it is very great indeed, and I suspect this is true for most of us who remember our childhood only as a long series of sharp private wounds covered with shame, anxiety, embarrassment. I knew only one truly happy family. Perhaps their story is worth telling.

I must begin at a strange place: a church rally for civil rights sometime in the early 1960s, where I had gone as an observer with the daughter and son of this family I should like to speak about. The daughter's name was Marguerita and the son was Andrew, and for years I had been a close friend of their parents'. Marguerita had been begging me to come to one of those rallies, as she was soon to go south as a voter registration worker and wanted me to overcome my reservations about this decision and fall in step with her enthusiasm. Marguerita was at that time about nineteen, and she held in my heart a place so flooded with warmth and feeling that I have only to think back on her bright smile, her warm vivacious looks, her incredible interest and enthusiasm, for something to break apart inside me. She was very fair; in fact it was impossible—if she did not with such bold enthusiasm constantly find ways to tell you—to know that she was Negro. Thick auburn hair, blue eyes, and clear radiant skin defined her as it did her mother, as if they were heirs of some magnificent Creole blood from which almost all Negro stock had been drained except a glow, a deepening that gave the skin its special radiance. Andrew was no less stunning: six feet tall at seventeen, muscular and imposing with curly black hair, bronze skin, and piercing light eyes that gave him an intimidating presence. Stunning children: loose, relaxed, sure of themselves and their world, full of humor, playfulness, a sense of responsibility to create a more just world. To be around them was to feel something so magical, so full of possibility, that even a heart as hardened as mine could only let go and believe.

When we arrived, Bayard Rustin was speaking—that veteran of so many battles and defeats—recalling to my mind so many early scenes of Pullman porters, Cuba, the Communist wooing of Negro intellectuals, that for a while I lost touch with Marguerita and Andrew and allowed myself the pleasure of my own memories. I don't know what called me back to the present, but when I looked up—speeches over, little groups of people assembling here and there to talk—I saw Andrew standing beside a young girl. I thought her frightened; I don't know why, but as sometimes happens to me, I had an almost immediate feeling about her and found my eyes riveted on the two of them: Andrew so sure and playful beside this intense girl, not pretty, not plain, only childlike and intense. I could tell he was teasing her; he loved to tease, his bright, charming personality swooping down with such force, such presence, I could see she hardly knew what to say. Then Marguerita came over and Andrew introduced them, and the three of them stood talking for quite a long time. Then I saw Marguerita looking around and I knew she was looking for me, so I quickly hurried over to them.

"Sorry . . ." I said, "you may not have converted me, but I've had a grand time remembering . . ."

"Did you like Julian Bond?" she asked. "And wasn't Forman terrific? You've got to understand now why I have to go . . ."

She was so intent on persuading me that she lost sight of the girl and Andrew, who were standing there, but just as sullenly she came back to them.

"Frank, you have to meet Christine. Andrew picked her up . . ." And she laughed with that infectious, delightful laugh of hers. "She's going to come spend the night with us and go back to school in the morning; it turns out she's going south this summer, too . . . I'm so excited I can't *stand* it. I thought I wouldn't know anyone and Andrew comes and meets the perfect person!!" And her excitement carried us all the way back to their apartment on Riverside Drive.

Lillie opened the door. If I take the same time describing the parents as I have the children, there's no way I shall not be accused of harboring incestuous impulses toward the whole family. And I stand quite willingly accused. For I surely carried a love affair with all four of them. Lillie had a face I never grew tired of watching. It had a kind of mobile beauty, serene, gay, straightforward, shy. Black hair like Andrew's, worn in a thick beautiful twist that let her elegant textures speak for themselves. She was slightly darker than Marguerita, a clear radiant bronze, and to be in her presence was to feel bathed in sunlight. Ralph, the father, and my longtime friend since childhood, looked every inch the serious handsome scholar that he was—at that time he was a professor of history at Columbia University. Light skinned with dark curly hair cut very short, glasses, a handsome nose and forehead that gave his face that serious scholarly distinction, but with such a warm, jovial sense of humor. Even now if I feel myself walk into that apartment, a sharp, painful nostalgia grips me. Life took on so much color you felt you were at the center of the universe, every good thing was possible, every good feeling was alive and well, every foolish part of yourself could come to the surface without fear of hurt or disapproval. It was marvelous. I tell you it was marvelous!

I remember how we sat around that night—late, late into the night—talking of civil rights, psychiatry, foolishness, music, commitment, freedom, poetry, dreams. One of those nights when talk spins a thick, womblike cocoon around the talkers and one grows drunk, ecstatic, joyfully sated with talk. When I left it was close to four. Lillie and Ralph were on their way to bed. Andrew and Christine were on the couch, still intensely involved in a conversation. Marguerita was dancing and listening to Billie Holiday sing "These Foolish Things." I walked home that night still full of talk—exuberant, palpable talk—still fresh and alive inside me. Lillie had been delighted to meet Christine, delighted to know that at least one other Negro girl of Marguerita's age would also be going south. And as the smallness of the world always has it, Christine's family were people both Ralph and Lillie had known for years. My mind flashed to a part of the conversation where Christine's bright and lucid mind swooped down, grasped the essential, and expressed it with such clarity and intensity that it surprised us. I saw her laugh. Not the hearty laugh Marguerita would add to a moment when she saw herself shine. But withdrawing with her laughter, withdrawing as if someone else had achieved that stunning and lovely synthesis of a complicated murdering conversation. It made me look at her. She wore her hair in two braids, no makeup, and while these things should have made her look young, they did not. She was the same age as Marguerita. They were both in fact college sophomores at the time, but there was absolutely no frivolity in her face. I have seen her recently, she is now a woman in her thirties and I find her quite beautiful. She still braids her hair and wears it up in some rounded soft fashion and she still does not wear makeup, but she looks like a young woman in her early twenties and her laughter is much freer. But when I first met her, she was not quite pretty, so stern and earnest were the contours of her face.

So Christine and Marguerita went south together. Andrew, at age seventeen, got on his three-speed bicycle and rode across the country, sending wonderful letters from Kansas, Oregon, New Mexico, California. Lillie would read them to me along with Marguerita's wildly enthusiastic prose about her experience in the South, how she was making contact with her roots, discovering a deep affinity and attachment to the soul of her people. What can I tell you that will allow you to see Lillie as clearly as I see her even now, poring over her children's letters, alive to every perception, every feeling happening to them. She herself had been raised in Boston, the daughter and granddaughter of DuBois-type revolutionaries. All her life she had been surrounded by ideas and the struggle to see them come into being. All her life she had felt herself a member of the elite, at the forefront of political and social change. And this feeling of being chosen, of being politically and socially responsible, she had passed on to her children. Marguerita followed quickly and eagerly in her footsteps. Not so Andrew, who had the poetic solitary bend of his father. Ralph, who would rather sit for days at a time and read a book, ponder an idea. Ralph, whose devotion to his children took the form of long camping trips in the woods, hiking, fishing, sailboating. Ralph, who took himself into analysis at forty years of age because he wanted to become a more sensitive, more open human being. But that is another story. Or is it another story? What detours must I take so that you might see the whole picture? I'd known Ralph for so many years. He was straightforward, ambitious, attracted to knowledge. He and Lillie married as soon as he came out of the navy in '42. He had none of the sure elitist instincts that gave Lillie her grace and charm. He was raised somewhere in southern New Jersey by working-class parents, and every achievement had been a struggle. Even at the time I am trying to recapture there were few Negroes in the academic world to which he belonged, and he suffered intensely from that, from the constant need to surpass, to be recognized and respected as a scholar. Ralph, who could distill from any experience a rich vein of humor and mirth and bring it home for his family to enjoy.

I don't think Ralph and Lillie loved each other. That is one of the small ironies I know I must communicate. I think they were, in fact, quite ill matched. I think Lillie was most likely cold. Sexually cold. And

I think Ralph had a repressed but basically passionate nature. Then how, you may ask, did they fuse such a truly magical and happy family? I don't know. Perhaps the outpouring of their love onto their children was the only real channel of discharge. Perhaps to love one's children one cannot be too obsessed, too absorbed, in the fulfillment of an adult love. I don't know. I only know that to walk into that apartment was to feel life brimming over, to breathe an air full of curiosity, honesty, a rich nurturing generosity to feel alive, happy, delighted with life.

Christine and Andrew fell in love. It was this event that became the focal point of everyone's attention from the moment the two girls returned from Mississippi. I was not surprised. Andrew had such an incredible presence that even I was often intimidated by him. He was one of those people whom you almost do not assign an age. He had the ability to focus himself on a moment, bring all his presence to bear and so charge the air that you were a bit shaken. Christine took to him like a puppy. Her whole face changed. Laughter crinkled the stern folds, shaking them loose for the first time. I carry with me always the memory of their young love. I would give anything to see them again, loose limbed and free, coming into that apartment and heating it up with a glow, an intensity so strong it made you tingle . . . mixed feelings ran through your mind . . . Oh my God, you thought, how life will take them apart, untangle them when they should be allowed to stay as they are, stay so deeply entwined, full of faith only in each other—oh, they should stay like that forever. I tell you in my mind's eye I have never let them change . . .

I met Christine's parents when the whole family was invited there to dinner, and they insisted I come along. Christine lived in a wonderful old rambling house in Connecticut. Her father was a politician, a member of the state legislature, and her mother a housewife. The atmosphere from the very moment you crossed the threshold was made of formidable stuff. Tight. Repressed. Robbed of that light, joyful spontaneity that is at the core of a happy family. Andrew almost walked out. He hated Christine's father instantly, his stern dominating manner, his well-bred but tight intellectuality. Christine was embarrassed. She wanted so much for her father to laugh, be gay; it was as if she were seeing her childhood for the first time with all its gloomy contours and she wanted so much for it to be otherwise. We left, all of us chastened but relieved.

For the full two years of Christine and Andrew's

love affair, Christine knew no peace from her family. They grew to hate Lillie and Ralph, consider them a corrupting influence on their daughter. They resented Andrew, scoffed at the difference in their ages, made Christine feel terribly guilty for abandoning them. Sometime she would come to the apartment, her face bloated and deformed from the stormy intensity of her family scenes at home. Her father was powerfully persuasive, and in his own domineering way deeply loved his daughter. But his only way of handling her rebellion was to crack down harder and harder, and this only alienated her still further. When she and Andrew separated—just around the time she finished college— she left the country and did not return for several years.

I did not mean to jump so far ahead. Christine was happy despite the stormy moments with her family. She and Andrew gave out such sparks that I know not what touchstones to leave with you. That magical Christmas we all went to Vermont and rented an old log cabin and tramped in the snow singing carols till we were hoarse; the bright nights before a roaring fire when talk glittered and glowed and I felt myself to be the luckiest person in the world; the races up and down Riverside Drive at four in the morning to clock the fastest time (Andrew always won); but if I leave you no other touchstone, please fix in your mind forever as it is fixed in mine that huge, wonderful living room overlooking the Hudson River high, high up on the twenty-third floor of an old New York apartment building. See Christine, her face so bright and childlike, held high in the air, her stomach flat against Andrew's feet, laughing a high-pitched giggle that I am pulling again from the past. See Marguerita in some crazy Gypsy outfit bringing in stray cats, laughing vigorously, and earnestly insisting that we all picket Chase Manhattan Bank at seven the next morning. See Ralph in the full early flush of his psychoanalysis, when he was sure he could cure himself of the double trauma of race and an overly stern and demanding mother. And Lillie. Living the brightness, the wild flamboyant charm of every hour, like a queen on her rightful throne. It was marvelous. I tell you it was marvelous.

And then it was gone. Andrew grew restless for life, and the age difference between him and Christine became a problem. He and Christine separated; she went to live in London. He roamed about, a poetic wanderer in search of elusive answers, refusing the discipline of college. Then one day the phone rang and he was dead.

A motorcycle accident in North Dakota. I must be telling this all wrong, for I can just as quickly finish up with Marguerita. She made a dreadful marriage at an early age to a man so poorly suited for her that he robbed her forever of her sparkle. And Ralph. A dreadful thing happened to Ralph. At a critical point in his analysis, his analyst died, leaving the very fabric of his personality asunder. No one could put it back together again. He is a man in shreds. And Lillie faded. Her children were the blood of that vital household that had fed the full flush of her personality, and when it collapsed she moved into the past and never left.

That is really all there is to the story. Why do I feel I have told it all wrong? Perhaps because I am not the one to tell it. I should let Lillie tell it, or Ralph, or Marguerita; perhaps they would add things that would put it all in clearer perspective. Tell you, for example, that their fair skin had something to do with it, that there is a racial dimension I have neglected to bring into focus; perhaps Ralph would say that no white man should attempt to tell it at all. This may be so. I'm quite willing to stand accused. But Lillie would be glad I told it this way, that I clustered the bright moments and made them shine. And it is only Lillie I am trying to please.

TREATMENT FOR A STORY

A ground-floor room in the back, cluttered with trunks, boxes, books, magazines, newspapers, notebooks, and paintings, and smelling of Gauloises, burnt coffee, dirty sheets, couscous and peppers, and a mélange of female scents. A window with bars opens on a courtyard. It's raining. A taxi pulls up in front. She gets out and runs inside. We wait. He comes out for her bags. The taxi takes off. He carries her suitcases inside. They embrace. He is wearing a maroon turtleneck that sticks to his skin and smells of damp sweat, and a pair of thin, pointed shoes that smell of casual sex (lightly exhaled, like cigarette smoke). He closes the door. It is raining a deluge. He puts her bags down (somewhere). They sit on the bed. The rain pounds away. She is thrilled by the dampness. By the cold and the clutter and the stale masculine swell. To which she adds her sex, her wet hair and an uncertain odor of eau de toilette. Heat rises from a pipe hung loosely between his lips and from intermittent grunts he emits during pauses in their conversation.

As if there were another conversation he was having with himself . . . Himself. While the rain pounds away. He goes out for food. She curls up in bed. Pulls the dirty sheets over her and starts to doze . . . Starts to doze until the room pulls her awake, overpowers her with its clutter, its scrawled notebooks and poems and letters to himself . . . Himself . . . The odor of his conversations gets under her skin, keeps her awake. As if she did not belong there. He returns. Heat rises from the sautéed pimento and peppers and the steaming couscous he prepares.

Heat rises from the burnt coffee he brings her. Heat rises. The stale masculine smell dominates everything. He lies down beside her. Now she can sleep. Morning. The room is deep and dark.

She goes out for a walk. Soaking up the fresh uncluttered smell that follows a rainy night. She walks and walks. She wets her tongue with the sharp licorice taste of Pernod. She sweetens her stomach with croissants.

Chauds. Avec du beurre et de la confiture. She looks for the sun cloistered in some lazy out-of-the-way garden. To fill her nostrils with flowers, warm dirt, wet blades of grass, and give her back the uncertain odor of eau de toilette. Then she returns to the ground-floor room. Where the rain beats down. Where she is overpowered by the casual scent of his thin, pointed shoes. By the scrawled odor of his notes and poems and letters to himself. Himself. Pounding the wet typewriter keys. Himself. Scribbling interminable notes. Himself. Extinguishing his pipe. She stretches out on the dirty sheets. He lights a Gauloise and lies down beside her. (It must be demanding and real, the odor he gives out. It must soak her up.) She takes her tongue and gently licks him, replacing the sharp licorice Pernod with the stale, sweaty taste of his body. Heat rises from his strange grunts. Heat rises. A triumphant commingling makes her spine tingle. Pure happiness. Her back arches. Pure happiness. A shudder overpowers her. She goes light. Pure happiness. A damp underground sleepiness takes over. It is raining in her dreams. The taxi pulls up and lets her out. She rubs her nose against a deep suede vest that smells sour and warm. Heat rises from the tinted neutrality of his gaze. He does not quite embrace her. He is busy scribbling a note. Rain pours down her back. Morning. The room is deep and dark. She goes out for a walk. Soaking up the sunlight. Relieving herself of the clutter. His clutter. She takes a deep breath and loosens her raincoat. She smiles at a stranger. She sips two *jus d'orange pressés*. *Oui. Deux.* And rolls the sweet taste around her tongue. Until she cannot go back again.

The rain does not let up. The scribbled notes get under her skin. All the heat is locked inside his strange grunts, his impenetrable conversations with himself. Himself. There is nothing to be gained there. Not even a hot shower.

STEPPING BACK

I'm not trying to flatter myself, but I was the first colored woman he ever seriously considered loving. I know I was. The first one who had the kind of savoir faire he believed in so devoutly. The first one with class, style, poetry, taste, elegance, repartee, and haute cuisine. Because, you know, a colored woman with class is still an exceptional creature; and a colored woman with class, style, poetry, taste, elegance, repartee, *and* haute cuisine is an almost nonexistent species. The breeding possibilities are slight.

I myself have never known another one like me, not one with my subtle understanding of art, music, drama, food, people, places, ambience, climate, dress, timing, correctness . . . whatever. As if all forms of cultural underdevelopment had somehow passed me by.

As if I took my racial heritage (so to speak) and molded it to my spirit . . . Then I emerged out of my cocoon like some new breed of butterfly.

I don't mean to go on like this, but when people say to me, "You don't know yourself to be colored! Don't you ever remember that you're black?" it makes me pause. I turn to my journal and devote pages to reminding myself that I am a colored lady. I try to bring myself up short. But again and again I am astonished at how uncolored I really am.

So I know it astonished him even more. At first he kept setting little traps for me. He would rattle on about Baudelaire and expect me to sit blankly by bobbing my head. He would lay out his best china and silverware and watch while I set the table for a formal dinner. He took me to chic little intellectual gatherings and watched for signs of slovenliness: overindulgence in laughter, incorrect pronunciation, insensitivity in a delicate and nuanced situation. Always in the end he was baffled and enchanted by the effortlessness of my style, its unself-conscious elegance and glow, fitting so neatly into his mid-Victorian life, fitting so undemandingly into his careful cultivation of an elegant colored life.

There had been white women, of course. But that was too obvious. A too-vulgar form of compensation. He did not like subjecting his cultivation to such overly sympathetic, such ingratiating discernment. The pain could destroy him, the humiliation crush a spirit already amputated by this reincarnation as a Negro. (Is it possible to imagine any greater amputation, any greater karmic debt, than reincarnation as a Negro? And to make matters worse, a Negro with aristocratic tendencies, left over, of course . . . there is always some residue carried over from life to life . . .) But white women were out.

Instead he cultivated a kind of boyish asexuality, charming to men and women alike. At our first meeting he charmed me, too. Adolescently debonair with his clear, lightly colored skin and his soft eyes . . . We lunched on the terrace of the Museum of Modern Art, allowing each other to perceive our distinctive tastes in books, films, music, theater, whatever. We smiled frequently at each other, as if there were sufficient grounds for a truce.

The following week he invited me to his home for dinner. I imagined a simple country place with rustic charm, perhaps a few stuffed moose over the fireplace.

Nothing could have prepared me for the splendor in which he lived. That he should pass his hours among marble ruins, Grecian busts, Italian neoclassical paintings, velvet mid-Victorian couches, Renaissance murals almost undid me. A hairsbreadth of a colored impulse escaped . . . I said, "Ain't this a blip!" but caught the words as they tumbled forth and coated them with charm. He appreciated the nuance and was delighted.

I made him Coquilles St. Jacques for dinner (with a bottle of 1970 Pouilly-Fuissé) and crepes filled with fresh strawberries for dessert. A Botticelli painting flickered elegantly in the candlelight.

After dinner we took a stroll through the gardens and down to the river. The moon was full. His black crinkly hair glistened. He seemed more debonair, more boyish than ever. We kissed. No unpleasant tongue-kiss, either. No over-moist search-and-seizure salivating the upper reaches of my throat. He focused on my lips, parted them softly, held them for a moment, then let go. Only to begin again this soft, effortless contact. We stood a long while under the trellis where yellow roses bloom in spring. Giving soft kisses.

It was delightful. Entrancing. Until my breasts began to tingle . . . I tried to imagine passing with him into the deep Heathcliffian gloom of his bedroom. I tried to imagine being lifted onto the splendid four-poster bed and undressed. My breasts stung and I longed to feel his fingers pull at them. Instead I caught myself stepping back . . . retreating . . . In the face of our delicacy, our . . . how could I occupy the splendid four-poster bed? Tastefully enough. How could I pass beneath the candelabras and undress? Tastefully enough. And make love? Tastefully enough? No colored woman could. No colored woman could. No colored woman could.

WHEN LOVE WITHERS
ALL OF LIFE CRIES

Listen, man. Listen. She said it was easy with me, that's all, just easy, she didn't have to lie, she could laugh instead, fall out in the street laughing, I wouldn't mind. It's true, man, as far as I'm concerned anybody can do anything, I don't mind, you want to make a fool of yourself I'll be the last person to stop you, you do it good I might even laugh. She could do it good, man, really double over and lose herself when she laughed. I liked to tickle her sometimes, make her yelp, but I couldn't believe one whole person could vibrate like that till the air shook. We were walking down the street one day and I told her I did two hundred sit-ups every morning as soon as I wake up. She reached out, touched my thigh, I pulled the muscles real tight and she swooned, I swear to God, man, fell out cold on the sidewalk in a swoon, opened her eyes and burst out laughing. Cracked me up, man. It was so absurd it snapped my mind, I pulled her up, crushed her so tight she yelped, I was so happy to have that moment. Okay, okay, she whimpered, wriggled free, and took my hand, okay, okay, what else do you do? Race up and down the bleachers at the track fifty times a day . . . I take her over there, she does five laps of cartwheels without stopping. Five times around the fucking track without stopping . . . hey, I kid you not, it was like watching the wheels of a bike spin in perfect motion, I almost came, man . . . not at first, no. She just brought in her portfolio like anybody else. I look at like three dozen a day, man. I take out *one* drawing, if it's not good I'd slip it back, thanks very much and good-bye, you know. Hers was birds circling around a cunt, breasts being pawed by scratches of hands titled something like *When All of Life Withers All of Life Cries*. Another one just a fuzz of lines, shoulders and head bent forward, arms pulling a baby with sweet genitals from between thick thighs titled something like *Birth Is the Only Renewal*.

Ricardo (straightforward): Your drawings are wonderful.

Miriam (clearheaded): They're good, yes . . .

Ricardo (amused): Oh, you know that already . . .

Miriam (clearheaded): I know how I feel when I do them. I only keep the ones that work.

Ricardo (straightforward): I can't see you working at a place like this; we've got the Gerber account, AAMCO Transmissions, Heinz ketchup. You want to draw for that kind of copy?

Miriam (defensive): I can do it . . .

Ricardo (clearheaded): I know you can do it; I am looking at your work, you can draw your ass off. That's not the point . . .

Miriam (laughing suddenly): Why do you look so sullen? . . . grouchy . . . like a dirty old man . . .

Ricardo (dry as a bone): That was totally uncalled for; you come in my office looking for a job and accuse me of harboring perverse wishes and dreams? . . . you'd last two months here. The first month you'd be dynamite, Gerber would never have it so good, and then you'd turn out the worst shit we ever saw. I'll take you to lunch . . .

Miriam (at lunch, in the middle of the story): . . . I'd never drawn before, but I took a piece of charcoal out of the stove and found some cardboard and I did them again and again. I figured out that I'd go crazy if I didn't draw. I was horny, it was freezing cold, too cold to sleep outside; during the day we found things to do, went hiking, tried skiing with a pair of makeshift skis we found in the cabin, but by five o'clock it was pitch-black out and freezing. We did fill the stove and have dinner, and then we did try to go to sleep. I'd pretend to be snoring because I knew they waited until they thought I was asleep to go at it, and one night I got the idea to draw them.

Ricardo (later on in the middle of the conversation about himself): . . . they left me alone, I roamed around a lot, stole fruit—only fruit . . . They saw I could draw early so I drew all the time, drew my way straight into advertising like some whiz kid, it came easy. I don't know why, though, because I've always had an attitude that made people uncomfortable. "Why don't you smile, man?" I must've heard that at least once every day of my life: "How come you never smile, man?" Even you called me sullen in five minutes. Like if you don't smile people can't get a fix on you. Don't get their daily quota of reassurance . . . You want me to smile, hit me with something fucking funny.

Miriam (walking Ricardo back to his office, in the middle of another story): . . . broken glass all over the place, nobody could fight like that, I couldn't believe it . . . I hate fights . . . fights and working both make me sick. Right away with fights; I can usually hold a job for a while before it gets to me, but one day I walk in the office and vomit. Sometimes I'll vomit four, five days in a row until I get the message and quit . . .

No, I saw her a lot after that. I called up a friend of mine at the anthropology museum and got her a job drawing skeletons. It's a low-key place, the hours are more flexible, and the work's always changing. No, man, she's not a hippie. Her old man shot himself four years ago, she's got two boys and an old barn of a house in Santa Barbara, and she likes to tell stories . . . about ladies who saw and men who did and children who didn't have—they could be tall tales full of shit, man, but the words are only icing; you keep going past the words you got nothing but surprises, a laugh like some happy bitch in heat, bright fingers weaving, cutting, flailing through the air, crinkly lines around the eyes and the mouth when she gets to the good part. Something warm, too, that you can smell right away . . . no, man, I ain't talking about fucking.

Ricardo (on the phone): I'd like to take you to dinner.

Miriam (clearheaded): All right, I'll have to get a baby-sitter. Could we eat late, around nine?

Miriam (at dinner, in the middle of a story): He always promised not to do it in the house and he kept that promise. They found him in the woods. I was so mad, I took my foot and kept kicking and kicking and screaming at him. I was sure I could bring him back if I screamed loud enough, kicked hard enough.

Ricardo (straightforward): Then what?

Miriam (shaking her head): We buried him, I carved his tombstone, a man and woman making love in a pile

of hay, because that's where it first happened, I wrote
DEATH IS NOT THE ONLY RELEASE . . .

Ricardo (later on, in the middle of a story): . . . it made
no sense, I cruised the whole island on that bike, going
up into the hills, coming down at breakneck speed,
rode all night until the sun came up and I fell asleep
on the beach. It was my kind of life, but I wouldn't let
myself have it, everything else makes me sullen, it's
true. Working for idiots who pay me fantastic sums
to sell dumb ideas, talking to people, that's the worst
part—I hate talking to people. That day it was clear I
should be off in Brazil climbing mountains, surf till
a wave snaps my neck, roller-skate down some endless highway, keep fighting with my body, that's the
only time I see clear . . . everything else makes me
sullen . . .

Miriam (moved): We're alike that way. I vomit, you get
sullen . . .

Ricardo (feeling at ease, drifting): One day I'd like to
paint, stop all this bullshit and just paint; it's the one
thing I won't do part-time, won't sneak in between

dumb copy and assholes, it has to be everything, I have to be able to do it all the time or forget it.

We had more in five minutes than in eleven years with Barbara. No, man, more . . . more guts, more life, more shit happening in the air between us, just more, man. If you've had less you know when you've got more, man. You say it out loud to yourself, "It's not just me, it's not just her, she's not backing away, I'm not backing away. It's a fuse; we touch the same wires."

Ricardo (straightforward): Can you spend the night?

Miriam (clearheaded): I can spend most of the night. I'd like to be home when the boys wake up.

Ricardo (straightforward): Fair enough . . .

Miriam (laughing): Fair enough, fair enough . . . everything about you is fair enough.

Ricardo (amused): Oh yeah, you think I'm funny. Sullen but funny. I crack you up . . .

Miriam (laughing . . . clearheaded . . . nervous . . . amused . . .): You have something direct and fair about you. It is fair enough; it won't hurt to take off my clothes, you have something so direct I . . . I haven't taken off my clothes for anybody in a long time . . .

Ricardo (straightforward): Fair enough; now come here and give up some of that cream . . .

There were times when we were just driving along in the car and she was telling me some story or other and I would start to sweat, get sopping wet from the tone in her voice. Man, absurd feelings for a life that had juice rang in her voice, my fingers kept slipping from the wheel, everything was serious, nothing was serious, everything was possible, life made complete sense because it made no sense but that was all right, it was enough, the tone of her voice was enough. No, Barbara and I were still together for a while there, there's no connection, man, for years I kept telling her things would have to change, she never worked, man, Chandra was already in school, there was always plenty of money, she got lazy, that's all, we had a good time for a long time and she got lazy, never got anything going for herself, kept to her mother and sisters, family gossip, family whims, family back-and-forth. It just went dead. There was no reason to stay, no reason to leave, either. She was always sweet and easygoing, there was just no reason anymore.

Ricardo (out of the blue): I didn't leave Barbara because of you . . .

Miriam (laughing): I never thought you did. That's got nothing to do with me. Maybe I'm a little interested in your daughter. I like kids; I don't like when they get fucked over by leave-takings . . .

Ricardo (blunt): I didn't leave my daughter. I got no plans to leave my daughter . . .

Miriam (seeing him clearly): Everything is serious to you. You don't just scowl all the time because you don't like to smile . . . everything is serious to you . . . really serious . . .

Ricardo (later on, in the middle of a story): My boss asked me if I could handle it another way, I said, "No, man, I can't deal with it any other way so I'm gonna play it the only way I know how. Take it to the street, man—you see him, you tell him I'll kick his ass, send him sailing twenty stories through the air," he was so scared he kept his office locked for a month . . .

No, man, she lives in Maine now, her family died and left her some money so she went back there, it's a big house, she likes that part of the country. Last summer she was here for a couple of months after the funeral, wrapping things up, trying to decide what to do.

Miriam (on the phone): Hello. I'm back . . .

Ricardo (straightforward): How'd it go? How are you?

Miriam (excited): I want to see you. Could we go for a swim tonight?

Ricardo (straightforward): No, tonight I can't.

Miriam (angry): How come you can't? Why don't you quit being so sullen and babble on a bit. Tell me why you can't!

Ricardo (straightforward but ignoring her): I'll meet you for a drink around five.

Miriam (stubborn): I don't want to meet for any damn drink. I want to go swimming with you.

Ricardo (stubborn): Then it'll have to wait till Saturday.

Miriam (angry): Why don't you give excuses, like you have to work late, like you're going on location, like you missed me and you're sorry you can't come rushing over. Why do you always have to be so fucking blunt?

Ricardo (straightforward): I'll see you Saturday . . .

Last week I was walking past a phone booth and I couldn't help going in and calling her in Maine. I wanted to tell her I was going to Brazil. She answered the phone almost right away and she was surprised. I was the last person she expected to hear from. She was almost angry but nice, flush, like she always was, full of questions.

Miriam (on the phone): What are you doing with yourself, are you painting, did you quit that dreadful job?

Ricardo (laughing): No, I didn't quit that dreadful job, but I'm taking a month off and going to Brazil.

Miriam (laughing): I hope you get lost in some damn jungle and can't get back . . .

Ricardo (dry as a bone): That was totally uncalled for . . .

Miriam (laughing): I do! I like to think of you painting to your heart's content in some little village, it'd be the best thing that could happen to you . . .

Ricardo (amused): What have you been up to?

Miriam (enthusiastic): I'm teaching the boys to sail and I've got a job, the sanest, craziest job I ever had; I draw animals for this company, I can stay home and draw as many animals as I want—birds, bears, orangutans—and once a week I turn in all the drawings. The man really loves my work, so he always takes at least one drawing a month to reprint and that gives me enough money above what my folks left. We live fine, the boys are happy, I'm happy . . . How was Japan? Did you think about quitting that lousy job and staying there? What are you doing with your life? You still surfing? You do any roller-skating? Why are you just going to Brazil for a month, why don't you go for a lifetime, start to paint . . .

I was holding on to her voice, man. She was angry with me; she didn't say it at first, just kept telling me how she was taking deep-sea diving and learning to do complicated etchings, how the boys had their first sailboat, and was I doing any surfing and what about roller-skating down that endless highway? She talked on and on, and I could feel the anger like she was slapping me across the face. You thought it could wait, it was so alive you thought it could wait, that it took no effort because you could laugh, talk, go inside, find pure cream waiting for you. You turned into a dumb motherfucker and switched track, agreed to go work in Japan for six months, backed away as if every day this came your way, every day you could touch, play, connect, make dumb jokes, absurd gestures, feel the fuse between us, what are you calling me now for? I saw it way back, I saw it, wanted it, waited around for you to see it, what are you calling me now for when it was right in the palm of your hand, damn it? "I'm glad you're doing great," I said, "I gotta run," and clicked the phone fast.

Miriam (after a swim, in the middle of a story): I never knew I had so many aunts, they all sat around the dining room with their rosy cheeks and thin hair sipping tea and greeting everyone who came. I'd forgotten I had a past, I walked around that house and saw how much it looked like my house, how I'd used almost the same wallpaper, the same colors, the same kind of furniture. I found Momma's old notebooks full of drawings, and I remembered how when we did something outrageous we'd come home, and hanging in the kitchen there'd be a caricature of me or my brother in some ridiculous pose that pointed a finger at what we'd done, I didn't even realize that I must have started to draw because my momma always drew . . .

Ricardo (straightforward): So it was a good experience . . .

Miriam (laughing): Yes, oh yes . . . it was a good experience. That sums it up brilliantly.

Ricardo (amused): Watch it now, before I . . .

Miriam (slipping between his legs and tripping him): Before you what, turn sullen and grouch? You ever hear yourself on the phone, how pissed off and ugly you sound? I missed you . . .

Ricardo (straightforward): That's nice . . .

Miriam (straightforward): I could live with you; I realized that while I was away, that I wished you were there, seeing everything with me.

Ricardo (straightforward): That's nice . . .

Miriam (straightforward): We could live together . . .

Ricardo (straightforward): I don't want to . . .

Miriam (angry): How come you don't want to? Why won't you give excuses like anybody else? Babble on and on about why you don't want to . . .

Ricardo (laughing but straightforward): I don't want to . . . What else is there to say?

I don't give explanations, man, that's something I've heard all my life, "Why don't you want to have Christmas dinner with the family?" "Why don't you want to go to the movies?" I just don't want to. Take the no and drop it. She could handle a no even if she did wince, she knew it was the only real answer. You want to do something or you don't. Reasons are like smiles, man, useless games people play. I don't know, man, I thought it could wait.

BROKEN SPIRIT

"I don't know how you survived! I've been all over this bloody country and I swear to God, I don't know how you survived! This place is a million godforsaken times worse than South Africa! Christ, man, apartheid puts holes in our dignity but it leaves us our culture, man! We've still got our lifeline, our traditions . . . Christ Almighty, man, they didn't leave you a bloody thing! Not a bloody thing! And to think I burned my bridges to come here! Jesus, God, what a bloody fix I'm in now!"

He was a journalist who came out of South Africa on a Nieman Fellowship to Harvard. We met at a party and he asked me to give him French lessons. So two afternoons a week we met in his room. Lovely afternoons. He was slippery and playful, and I had to tease him into speaking. "I can't speak that bloody language," he'd say, and laugh and dart around the words and make fun of me. That's how we became friends.

He was frequently away on a story, but it got so he'd call when he came in even if it was three or four in the morning, and I'd get in my car and go over. I'd come in the door and he'd start to tease me about how all "educated female American colored ladies" should emigrate to Swaziland. "I know hundreds of girls like you," he'd say, "and they're not neurotic and lonely like you ladies over here."

"All right," I'd say, laughing, "I'm leaving soon," and we'd talk about South Africa. Sometimes if he'd been drinking he'd rant on a bit, even cry, and I knew then how much he missed it, how much he regretted giving it up to come to this "fucking stale place," as he put it. And he could put it so well in his cool, aloof English, walking back and forth drinking and fumbling on about "this bloody place" that was breaking his spirit and "what a bloody fucking mess" he'd got himself into now, and "what the bloody hell" was he supposed to do but "bloody well beg for mercy without a bloody fucking passport to go anywhere else." Then we'd go to bed when the light was coming up.

Sometimes I felt like we made love inside a vacuum that must have been his loneliness. Sometimes I felt like we were inside his cool, graceful humor. Only once did I feel we broke all the way through to each other.

Then I moved to Vermont for the summer and left him my address. I had an apartment over an old barn. I like the mountains and the woods, and I like to swim in the cold water from the gorges and lie on the rocks for hours reading.

One morning I got up and went to pick up my paper so I could browse through it with my coffee, and I got stopped on a page, on a name . . . it couldn't be his name . . . on a death . . . it couldn't be his death . . . "If I should learn, in some quite casual way, / That you were gone" . . . jumped from a twentieth-story window, say . . . "I should not cry aloud—I could not cry / Aloud." Oh no, I said. You didn't do that. You couldn't have done that. No, I said, you didn't go and do that. You couldn't have. And I choked on his death, on his cool, aloof self, refusing to live with a broken spirit. No, my friend, you didn't go and do that . . .

DOCUMENTARY STYLE

I spent ten years in the navy before I came to New York City to be a filmmaker. When I got out I was badass and feeling sorry for myself, but I was also thinkin' I was the best goddamn black cameraman to hit New York. My body was tight from years of karate and I could handhold a camera, pan, tilt, track, like a motherfuckin' dancer. I knew I knew more about filmmaking than most of those dudes coming out of the film schools and I was gonna make me some films!

I got a job with this black dude who had his own company; he'd spent his ten years in exile, too, learning his craft, so I thought we might see eye to eye. I was impressed with his credentials and wanted to show him what I could do.

He took me on location as a second unit man under

this white dude whose footwork I knew was no better than mine; I was tight, but I was gonna shoot some motherfucking films and show his ass. It was a training film on sensitizing white employers to their black employees, so we got everybody talking together in a room and turned on the cameras. I was supposed to do the pickups, but at the last minute my boss decided to go with one camera and keep my hands busy in the changing bag. I was tight; I watched that white dude pussyfoot around, bending his knees and squintin' . . . How come he had to circle so much? I knew there was more economy in my moves, and why was the camera on now, anyway? Nothing was happening. The ice was cold between those suckers. I pulled my boss over to the side and suggested that the dude just pretend to be shooting, but keep the motor off until he felt some heat between the men. He waved his hand and almost laughed at me with some off-the-wall explanation about how he always shot a lot of footage because you could never tell when the moment might happen, and besides it was good to have a lot of atmospheric stuff to play with in the cutting room. My hands were burning up the changing bag.

I asked if I could shoot the black dudes alone in

the barroom, using as a rationale how they'd be much looser around me and give off more juice. He let me know it was already in his head to do just that, but he was glad we were thinking along the same lines. He had a way of addressing you like he knew from the get-go that you couldn't be much above a pile of shit. But I knew I was bad. That bar sequence was gonna smoke! He wouldn't need to hire more white dudes after that.

We set the place up good. Low-keyed lights (I placed them myself). No distortion. Natural feeling. I let the dudes establish the rhythm. One cat turned out to be a natural comedian. He told this story about how on a job his boss finally said to him, "Boy, you ain't puttin' out that quality work like you used to . . ." "That's 'cause you ain't puttin' out that quality pay like you promised me . . ." I was dancing! Got him. Got the dudes reacting to him. Got it. Got it.

We hit the cutting room and I couldn't wait for the cat to see my shit. I came in early and there was this chick bent over the Moviola. Legs and more legs, and when she turned around a little fat belly about six months on. Light skinned to high yaller but with nice eyes. She was his assistant editor so she was synching my shit. I introduced myself. I had a thing against light-skinned chicks. I asked her how much footage she'd synched. She said she was just getting started.

The boss came in and asked if we'd met. He told me I should work with her on the synching and he'd come look at it when it was ready. What the fuck was he doing puttin' me in the goddamn cutting room with some smart-ass high-yaller chick? There was another Moviola in the other room, so I picked up some footage and split. "You ain't puttin' out that quality work . . ." She was not gonna synch my shit.

I got one roll ready and asked the boss to come take a look. He wouldn't. Said he liked to screen everything together so he could get an overall view of the piece. I wanted the dude to know what a bad motherfucker he'd hired!

It wasn't until Thursday that he sat down to screen the stuff. The white dude's stuff was all right. No shakes. Smooth. But to my eyes it looked flat, like he wasn't really involved. Then the bar stuff came on and I knew he was gonna flip. A little shaky here and there where I got too excited; I'd tried some quick zooms and didn't correct focus fast enough. But it had an arty feel to it. It was alive. It caught the dudes in heat.

He never said a word. Just told the chick to send the stuff out for coding and they'd start cutting next week. I asked him how he felt about my work, and he patted me on the shoulder and told me I'd get there. With a little work and a little patience I'd get there.

The chick came into my room to catalog my footage. I told her I'd send my stuff out for coding. She told me that was her job 'cause she knew how he liked things numbered. I told her any asshole could number the shit. She said maybe so, but she thought she should do it. I told her what the fuck was so complicated about sending the shit out for coding. She said there was nothing complicated about it, she just had to assign the right numbers to the rolls. I told her any asshole could do that. She said maybe so, but she'd still better do it herself. I said shit, woman, who the fuck do you think you're talking to, and she said she knew who she was talking to and she was just trying to get the stuff out for coding. I said get the fuck out of my room. She said she would if I'd give her the footage and she would catalog it in her room. I said get the fuck out of my room. She said she would if I would please give her the footage and she would catalog it in her room. I said get the fuck out now. She said she would if I would please give her the . . . I gave her my foot karate chopped right in her fucking fat stomach and told her who the fuck did she think she was fucking with 'cause I was the best fucking goddamn black cameraman in this country and I'd walk all over her before I'd give her my footage to code.

LIFELINES

I was in a mess. My husband was gone. He now lived somewhere in Santo Domingo, a place I'd never been to in my life. He'd taught himself Spanish, Portuguese, Arabic, German, French, Italian, and Creole, and he could live anywhere in the world and be happy. I couldn't. But I'm not at all sure that was the reason for our discontent.

It's difficult to sort things out. For instance, before he left for Santo Domingo he'd been in jail for a year on a charge of fraud (involving stocks and bonds and commodities and options and options on commodities and . . . I'm still in the dark about the nature of the charge). He'd been confined at a maximum-security prison that was shockingly overcrowded; violent eruptions of one kind or another were a daily occurrence.

He was in a constant state of shock and desperation. Every day when his letters came I thought my heart would break.

Dear C—

Some days I wake up and I no longer know who I am, I cannot imagine any past before yesterday and it seems that all my life I have been awakened at five A.M. to the dreadful blare of loudspeakers and the frightening presence of seventy-five other desperate . . .

His letters put me in such a state I would fly upstairs to my typewriter and pound out a letter that might hold him for just a moment longer.

Dearest . . .

You sound discouraged beyond belief. I can't bear it when you sound like that. I know that life is a hellhole for you now. I know, too, that there's no way in the world for me to understand the hourly horror and humiliation and fear you live with. What can I say to make it all right, what can I say that will make you want to hold on and live . . .

I did everything I could to make his days more bearable. I spent all my spare moments in bookstores, at foreign newsstands, or in the library looking for interesting books, magazines, or periodicals to distract him.

Dearest . . .

I'm sending along some things that should bring you a little pleasure. I've packed them in different envelopes and I'm mailing them one day apart so you can look forward to several packages. In one I've sent you Kierkegaard's *Fear and Trembling* as you asked, and with it I sent this month's *Esquire, Playboy, Oui, Players,* and *Town & Country.* In another I put *Swann's Way* and *The Sweet Cheat Gone,* along with *One Hundred Years of Solitude.* The third envelope has those Portuguese grammar and conversation books you wanted, along with several Portuguese magazines and periodicals, and yes, *Le Nouvel Observateur* is in that package, too, and the last envelope has a book of Éluard's poems along with this week's *New Republic, New York Review of Books,* and *Century.* Oh, and I did order your subscription to the *Catholic Worker,* to be sent to you directly there. You should begin getting it in a few days. Last week I played five concerts back-to-back . . .

Dear C . . .

I'm so pleased to have *Fear and Trembling*, it speaks to me in a way I never expected. Yesterday was a very strange day. I was unloading boxes in the warehouse when a flock of birds went by on the platform a few feet in front of me. I suddenly recalled that long boat trip we'd taken to Cyprus when it rained and the sky was dark with birds and the sea was so unbelievably rough we were sure we were done for. I don't know why but the memory was so clear as if it were happening that very instant and it seemed to reassure me of something. I had the definite feeling that I would make it, and later when it was mail call a letter arrived from you that touched on the same memories and I felt you must be very close to my thoughts. When you have a chance will you send me that Arabic dictionary? . . .

Dearest . . .

I just got your letter where you talk about remembering our trip to Cyprus. I don't know why it made me cry, perhaps because we have known so many cruel years recently together. It's almost as if your time in jail is the first lifeline back to happier times, but mostly I'm glad it gave you strength. It makes me want to put down all those wonderful memories just so you can feed off them and hold on to them, and this way we can blot out all the bad years because they can only discourage you now and only what is best between us is meant to survive and pull you through these strange days. I mailed the Arabic dictionary along with an odd little book of Arabic poetry, and I also enclosed a series of articles from the *Times* on Puerto Rican poets and playwrights . . .

I felt like I was in prison, too. I lived only for the mail. It was our conduit. What it brought and what it took away gave the only possible spark to a day. When a letter didn't reach us we would both panic and time would stop till the next delivery.

At the end of the tenth month he was released early for good behavior. When they brought him over from the island I was waiting to take him home. He was shockingly thin and his hair was extremely short. His eyes were frightened and his body had a tense, nervous quality that made me hurt.

But we had nothing to say to each other. We had said it all. The best, most complete expression of our relationship had just come to an end. Through our letters we had cleared up the odd inconclusive bits and pieces of a relationship that had never led to ful-fillment. Through our letters we had forgiven each other our disappointment. Through our letters we had taken the best parts of our affection and caring and used them in the defense of his sanity and whole-ness. Face-to-face we were now more than strangers. I felt only relief when a few weeks later he boarded the plane for Santo Domingo, Chile, Brazil, wherever his hunger and thirst for something new might take him.

I was not prepared for the desolation that soon settled over me and left me in a mess. I would wake up crying. I felt old. Useless. Sick at heart as if my life was draining away and I hadn't the strength to call it back. I felt no connection to anyone, not even to my violin (I'm a violinist with the New York Phil-harmonic).

I left the city and went to stay in the small cabin we owned in the Adirondacks. Sporadic letters would reach me from somewhere in South America.

Dear C—

There's a zillion things to say, to tell about, but one thing is incredible—I've just been to Carnival in Rio and it's unbelievable. *Black Orpheus* is like a first outtake—there is no way to really describe it, it just goes on and on, day and night, there is no end to the exhilaration, the dancing, the drums, or the hundreds of bands marching through the streets, the crowds so thick you are carried by them, the colors that blind you—your body gets exhausted and you try to put more rum into yourself to sustain you, you're ready to drop from dancing, your senses are worn out—shit, I can't talk about it now, it is still too close.

All this is to say I am alive (a million thanks for the bread!)—plans are still open . . .

His letters made me tired. I wanted no news, no information, no pictures. I wanted the connection to slip. Sever itself. Cease to pull and tug at me in a vague, empty way.

I went into town one day to have my hair cut. The hairdresser I normally used was no longer there. Instead they gave me a new woman. She wore glasses. I don't remember anything else about her except her voice, which was tiny. She spoke as if she were afraid of words. "How shall I cut it?" she asked, gripping each word and holding it between her teeth.

"Oh, just cut it fairly short and part it to the left, I just want it out of the way," I answered. I could no longer see myself. One adornment was as valid as another.

She worked carefully and I noticed she was cutting off very little. My old self would have protested, but now it mattered so little to me; I let her do as she pleased. It wasn't until she was putting in the rollers that I felt her hands shake a little. The rollers kept slipping and falling to the floor.

"Oh my . . ." she said, like a bird who sensed it was going to fall from its nest. "Oh my, you're standing in front of a white house, it sits way back from the road and it has shutters, it's small . . ."

I didn't know what she was talking about, but her fingers made gentle traces through my hair as if she were drawing a map of what she was seeing. "Oh my . . . It's been so long since I've seen anything; why, it's *your* house," she chirped, "it's your house, oh, it's very sunny inside and you'll be happy there . . . You won't meet him at first, he only comes on weekends."

I started to cry. I had no idea what this bird-like woman was talking about, but I went to pieces. Sorry . . ." I said, when I realized I must be making her uncomfortable.

"It's all right," she whispered. "It's all right . . ."

"I'm just tired, too many things have been happening lately and I haven't been able to sort them out."

"It's all right . . ."

"You think you've done the right thing," I said, feeling a terrible need to go on, "but then it gets so empty all of a sudden and you don't know why."

"Yes . . ." she said, and I knew if I didn't stop I'd go to pieces again.

It began to rain the next day and it rained for the rest of the week. I went back to the city out of desperation and took a job playing with an off-Broadway musical. A letter arrived from Jamaica.

Dear C—

I'm somewhere in the middle of Kingston, but I'm surrounded by foliage and I'd never know it. In the distance, all around the Kingston basin, are postcard mountains, very green with fog hanging over them. It's about 80 and breezy, and I'm staying in a guesthouse not far from M——and his girlfriend. I may end up taking a job here as a liaison man for a firm that works back and forth between here, Santo Domingo, and Venezuela. Might settle in Santo Domingo because I like it better. We'll see . . . You can write me here c/o the American embassy. How goes it . . .

Dearest—

Every time I turn around you're someplace else! Are you ever planning to stay put? You mention perhaps settling for a bit in Santo Domingo. Is that real? Do you need any money? I am playing with some dumb off-Broadway musical but it's all right. The city is hot. I'll go back up to the cabin soon. How're the headaches? Going away, I hope. You sound more and more like yourself again, and you're seeing so many wonderful places and things. I am really glad. Are you sure you don't need anything?

When the musical ended I decided to go back to the cabin. I ran into an accident on the thruway and traffic was backed up for miles. I detoured onto the Palisades and thought I'd go up 9W. It was a lovely day and I was in no hurry. I stopped in a little town near Garrison for lunch, when I remembered that we used to have friends in this area, a couple we'd known when we first got married and whom we'd frequently visited in the early days. I tried to find their house. I knew it was near a stream and an old church set back from the road. I finally found it.

The wife came to the door. She'd changed a great deal, but then I thought I might have, too. She was alone; the marriage hadn't survived and she was yearning to get away, move somewhere else, start a different kind of life, but she had to find a buyer for the house before she could leave.

Out of the blue I offered to live in it until it was sold. I don't know why I made that offer, the idea just came upon me like that—it suddenly seemed the answer to my restlessness. I wanted to be out of the city for a while, but the cabin was just too far for commuting. I'd always liked their house; it was an easy fifty minutes from the city. Somehow it made sense.

I have a clear memory of the first night I spent in that house because it was the first time I had felt at peace with myself in so long. The house suited me. It was small and the sun came into every room, filling it with light and giving me an incredible sense of well-being.

Dearest—

I'm living in Buzz and Janet's house upstate. You remember when we used to come up here a lot? It's a long story. They split up, and somehow I'm staying here until it's sold. It's a nice house and I'm liking the change. The cabin is so far. Have you found a place yet? The job sounds wonderful. I'm really happy here, it's such a nice change for me . . .

I knew no one else in the town other than the few introductions Janet made before she left. But one day I ran into a musician with whom I frequently played and he turned out to be a near neighbor. He and his wife invited me to dinner. It was the most relaxed evening I'd spent in years. I was happy. A real life seemed possible again.

A few weeks later the real estate agent found a buyer. I was shocked. I couldn't leave now. I couldn't imagine going back to my old life. I called Janet and asked if we could possibly come to some understanding. Several weeks went by in a state of indecision, but finally she made it possible for me to buy the house under reasonable terms. I was going to own the house; I couldn't believe it!

The night of the closing I was ecstatic, and my musician friend and neighbor invited me to dinner to celebrate. A gentle-looking man whom I'd never seen before was among the guests. We were introduced. He came infrequently, it was explained to me, because he had to spend a great deal of time on the West Coast, but he actually owned the house next to theirs and came home as many weekends as he could. It was a lovely evening, heightened for me by the unbelievable fact that I now owned the house!

The next morning brought a letter from Santo Domingo.

Dear C—

That's really great about the house, though I have a hard time imagining you as a homeowner. How much land do you have? Anything I could speculate with? How does it work anyway, am I a partial absentee owner as your husband? I'm living in a cabana on the beach for a while, but I'd like to find a place up in the Red Hills. This job could lead to something interesting, I might even end up in Brazil again speculating in copper futures, we'll see. Did you forward those boxes yet . . .

The letter bothered me. He had no right to think of himself as a partial owner of my house; it was like being held by a thread that kept me in the shadows. It threw out a vague lifeline that insisted I was still in his life but not really in his life, that my existence somehow fed a need in him for a symbiotic wife who would always be there if a lifeline was ever needed. But it wasn't a *real* link; it could never nourish me. The connection was too thin.

A few weeks later I was invited again to dinner at my musician friend's and the same man was there. We talked slightly. I was attracted to the silence about him. Late the next afternoon he called and we talked for quite a while. He was on his way back to the West Coast.

Dearest—

I think I should sell the cabin. It would give us both a little free money. What do you think? I'll keep it, of course, if you imagine yourself one day wanting to be there again. Let me know . . .

Dear C—

I think you're right, it should be sold. The cash

would be great if I decide to invest in a little property down here. I hate to give it up, though. I hate to give up anything that belongs to my past, it feels like I'm burning old love letters or tearing up old photographs, it gives me a wrench. But do what you think best . . .

I went up one weekend to place it in the hands of a real estate agent. She saw no difficulty in selling it quickly. It was in excellent condition, was not too expensive, just the kind of weekend retreat someone would snatch up quickly.

When I got home Sunday evening the phone was ringing.

"Hello," I answered, a bit out of breath.

"Hello, I've been trying to reach you all day . . ." he said.

"I'm sorry, I was away all weekend . . ." I answered.

We talked briefly. He was on his way back out to the West Coast. It wasn't until a few weeks later that we spoke again.

He called on Friday and asked me to the gallery opening of a painter friend of his that was being held in the next town. After the opening we had dinner and sat and talked a long time. Saturday afternoon we went canoeing in the stream behind his house and later sat in his big, sprawling kitchen and drank wine and talked. I was happy.

When I woke the next morning I was caught in the meshes of an odd dream about the hairdresser I'd been to in the Adirondacks. She had come to visit me and I was showing her through the house, and I kept saying to her, "Just wait, at any minute the sun will come out and you'll see how much light it gets." And we kept walking from room to room, waiting for the sunlight, and I was getting more and more impatient because I wanted her to see the house filled with light. When I woke the contours of the dream were still clear and they suddenly threw me back to that afternoon when she was cutting my hair and talking about a house. It was my house! I jumped awake. It was *my* house! She'd talked about a white house with shutters that sat way back from the road and was very sunny . . . it was *my* house! She'd described my house, and I felt turned inside out. Like my life was tracing a clear, inevitable path that had nothing to do with me, that the twists and turns that had brought me to this place had come about because some birdlike lady with glasses had traced them into my hair!

I wanted to see her again. The cabin was just about sold and I had a lot of last-minute cleaning to do anyway. I went up the next day.

When I walked into the beauty parlor she was shampooing someone's hair. I walked up to her, friendly and excited.

"Hello," I said, "I was in here several months ago but I'm sure you'll remember me. You traced my future in my hair . . . you saw me in a white house with shutters that sat back from the road, a small house with lots of sunlight, and you said I would be happy there and I would meet someone who came on weekends . . ."

"Oh, that's nice . . ." she chirped, still gripping each word as if it would break apart before she could finish with it. "That's very nice."

"Do you remember?" I pursued. "You were putting in the rollers and your fingers started shaking . . ."

But she didn't remember. All of a sudden I knew she didn't remember a thing. It was like music, a dance, an exquisite sonata performed one time only and never recorded. It was my music, my dance, my sonata that had put my life on its own path. And a queer, old, birdlike lady had played it before me.

OF POETS, GALLERIES,
NEW YORK PASSAGES

"What did he look like then? Like an Irish poet, thin, dark curly hair. He was always broke. Always running around Paris borrowing money from someone in the Sixteenth Arrondissement. He was handsome. Remarkable for his suits, his elegant open shirts, a thin little mouth that spoke a good spattering of any language on any subject. Considered witty. He was certainly considered witty. Always in good taste . . ."

They were sitting around the dinner table in a huge Soho loft. One of those former machine shops now stripped, windows thrown open to the sun, ingenious rooms carved out of cavernous space, a cozy kitchen with clever cupboards. Something rough, still, in the walls; the too-abundant space concealing old sprinklers and untidy ceilings. There were three of them: Ellen, who tomorrow would have her first one-woman show; Mickey, a painter of reasonable standing though remarkable talent; Louise, a friend from the country. The friend to whom they constantly referred was Edouardo, who had come to dinner the night before and slapped Louise rather viciously across the face.

"He's become quite mad," Mickey said, "though he's always had it in him. Once, in Paris, he chased me out of a restaurant for some chance remark that offended him. Caught up with me and clawed my face with his nails." He smiled at Louise. "But you, why you've always been the princess for him, it's always Louise who can do no wrong. He keeps you fresh. Like the one unsoiled memory dating all the way back to Paris. 'Louise became something . . .' that's his favorite way of putting it . . . 'Louise became something.' "

Ellen laughed. Her laughter had the irrelevant taint of a stranger to the past. As indeed she was. Her affection for Mickey was the only link to the trio that held between them common memories of fifteen-odd years of friendship. "Edouardo's a shit," she said. "I know you forgive him because you remember the curly hair, the elegant poverty-stricken days, but really he's a shit."

"A shit . . ." Mickey said, giving the idea careful consideration. "Do you agree?" he asked Louise.

"He used to write poems." Louise sighed.

"Aw, come off it, honey," Ellen said, and laughed. "No one's ever seen a line! Oh, he drops his little hints. When he's in one of his sensitive moods he alludes to quiet meanderings down poetry lane, and I say, 'Listen, Edouardo, one of my real pleasures would be to read a bit of your quiet verse, I'd love it, believe me, I'd love it.' Then he sighs. 'Yes, perhaps one day we shall,' he says, and folds that subject neatly back into his too-tight pants."

"Ellen can be a bit rough when it comes to Edouardo," Mickey apologized, hugging Louise. "Listen, Louise, have you any idea how good it is to see you? You never set foot outside that happily-ever-after in suburbia, and here we've got you for three whole days in New York. You'll see Ellen's show, we'll smuggle you in and out of a few choice bars, we'll try to overlook last night's brutal mugging. How's your eye?"

"I can feel it," Louise answered gently.

"You look good," Mickey soothed, "you look young with your five children, your poems and plays, you have the fertile look of someone happy-ever-after . . ."

"You've really got this thing about my living in the country." Louise laughed.

"It's so healthy, it reeks of healthiness: fresh air and trees, little budding brooks and howling children . . ."

"I have nowhere *near* five children," Louise insisted.

"But you're always producing . . . books, plays, children . . . all you do is sprawl out under trees and breed." Mickey laughed.

Louise smiled. "You're just attached to this idea that I lead a simple existence—"

"Listen, dearie," Ellen interrupted, "you should hear Edouardo on the subject of your graceful existence. 'Louise has achieved a life . . .' that's one of his favorite expressions about you . . . 'Louise has taken the measure of things and achieved a life.' " She lit another cigarette.

She was a short, dark woman with ravenous eyes and the stubby, fat fingers that often belong to painters. There was almost a physical resemblance between her and Mickey. He, too, was short, with pale, scruffy good looks, a boyish affect, brash and intent. Beside them Louise had a handsome, placid surface.

Mickey hugged Louise again. When he was a little drunk his affectionate need to touch and handle became more intense. "You're so fertile, I feel if I squeeze you too hard you'll reproduce right here at the table."

Louise burst out laughing. "What a lot of ideas you hang around me . . . Why do you burden me with your ideas about me?"

"You don't admit you're fertile," he insisted.

"I'm not a cow." She laughed again.

"Then you refuse to acknowledge a certain pastoral earthiness," he persisted.

"Good God," Louise cried, "I'm just an old friend who happens to live in the country. Perhaps I'm a shade more at ease than I might be if I still lived in New York."

Louise lowered her head and drank her wine. Mickey continued to stare at her with intense affection. Ellen busied herself preparing Turkish coffee and dessert.

"Tell me more about Edouardo," Louise asked quietly.

"There's the museum," Mickey answered. "Everyone says they'd like to drop him but they keep him on as fourth curator or some such nonsense. He's invited to the right openings."

"Usually with Henrietta," Ellen added.

"He's made a bit of a name for himself," Mickey continued. "He collects paintings. Does it with a bit of splash, too. He's got a few of mine. Two of my best, in fact."

"How do you feel about his owning your work?" Louise asked.

"He makes a very big deal about it," Mickey answered irritably. "Don't misunderstand, other people buy my work, but with him I'm forced to remember it—frequently."

"Edouardo tallies things up," Ellen said.

"Listen, if he doesn't buy something from your show you'll be in a state," Mickey said to her.

"Not quite that intense," Ellen answered. "It's Ricardo who's counting on it."

"Ricardo's her gallery owner," Mickey explained to Louise. "They're like high-class salesmen . . . Art has become a fashion show: chic openings, brittle cocktail parties—the decorative impulse reigns." He looked at Ellen. "I'm not talking about you . . . Her work is good, the real thing," he said to Louise. Then he raised his glass. "A toast to Ellen's show. It's a good gallery and that still means something in New York."

Ellen waved her glass in the air. "It means all the parasites came out to suck your blood, dearie, that's exactly what it means."

"You're tough," Mickey said to her. "She's a tough lady," he added to Louise.

"Look who's talking"—Ellen laughed—"the Lone Ranger of the art world!"

Mickey lunged forward into Ellen's face. "Is that how I'm regarded?"

"That is exactly how you're regarded and you love it." Ellen laughed again.

"She thinks she knows me," Mickey said to Louise. "She's a witch . . . though it's true I'm not interested in fashion."

"Nobody could accuse you of that, dearie," Ellen said. "All those stubborn little fingers know how to do is paint well. He's a genius," she added to Louise.

"And she's a witch." Mickey laughed, a raucous undercurrent of wine-sated delight taking hold. "I'm in the presence of two abundantly fertile women," he roared.

"Oh God," Ellen groaned, "I feel like a giant duck . . ." Louise broke into hysterics. "Can you believe this routine?" Ellen said to her. The women giggled.

Mickey stared at them as if at some dazzling unknown species. "Look at the two of you," he fairly shouted, "you create, you breed, you smile, you even hold on to your glamour."

"And at midnight we turn back into witches." Ellen chuckled.

"We make wonderful photographs." Louise bowed luxuriously.

"Listen, dearie," Ellen continued, "I bet right now Edouardo's got that fast left to your eye incarnated in same delicate lyric sonata."

"The light that fell on Louise is gone." Louise flourished dramatically.

"A fitting epitaph to your fall from grace," Ellen approved, and the women laughed outright.

Mickey continued to stare at them with fascination. "You've had husbands," he suddenly said.

"We have!" they chimed back instinctively, overcome by a kind of giddy inexplicable hysteria.

"Yours was a poet," Mickey said to Louise.

Louise nodded. "With one of those handsome abstract faces that go well with poets. You once told Edouardo you didn't approve of my husband," she said, and giggled.

"He told you that?"

"Over one of those dinners where he was concerned about the state of my life he said to me, 'Mickey has never approved of your husband.' "

"And how did you feel about that?"

"It struck me. Edouardo has a way of declaring his opinions, and obviously he shared that one. As though they were facts and everything should change accordingly. In a word, it was time I divorced my husband at once."

"But you didn't."

"Not for many years . . . though it was soon after that I decided to move to the country."

"And began the life that Edouardo so admires."

Louise smiled. "It isn't a lie."

"Louise lives on excellent terms with her solitude." Ellen giggled.

"Is that Edouardo talking?" Louise laughed.

"As close as I could get without him walking through that door . . ."

"I'm a photograph . . ."

"Royalty . . ."

"But I've got a black eye!"

"Louise has achieved a certain humility." Ellen bowed grandly. "It was time for Louise to achieve a certain humility . . ."

DEAD MEMORIES . . .
DEAD DREAMS

1

The H_____ clan is the one mythical spot on my land-scape, a reminder that I'm at the tail end of a queer inbred strain. My mother, dead Lillie, was the first to marry outside the clan, so she gave me an outsider for a father. But her own blood was so diluted she lasted not much longer than the time it took to put me in the world.

To the H_____ people I'm an outsider, not full-fledged; my father's darker blood runs in my veins and my skin is a clear shade off. At funerals and weddings and all gatherings of the clan, one is surrounded by pale, anemic-looking Negroes, pasty skin the color of lightly scorched sugar. Eyes washed cloudy blue. Slight

southern twang when they speak, and something alto-
gether too queer about the whole persona.

"My, my, Lillian," they say to me, "you've grown,
the child has grown." Then they chuckle. "But she
didn't get no lighter . . ." And they chuckle again.
"How's your father," they shout, "still moving all them
bodies around?"

Besides being too brown, my father compounded
his sins by choosing the most colored occupations.
Undertaker. Mortician. Funeral director. Keeper of
the dead.

"That's why dead Lillie's dead," they shout. "You
watch over 'em long enough you turn into one of
'em . . ."

They blame my father for dead Lillie's death. "Your
father had Rosie's Lillie [Rosie is my grandmother who
tried to keep me when dead Lillie died but who lost
in court to my father] stashed away on the third floor
while he was down below bringin' bodies in and out,
he had her sittin' by the phone waitin' for somebody
to call up dead and ask for the hearse to be brought
'round for them, that's how he made her live, when the
child was used to Rosie and her silks and wallpaper
and cherry furniture . . . but there she was playin' sec-

retary to the dead. She didn't die a natural death, she was tired of sittin' . . . no furniture but the telephone, bills only more dead bodies could pay, a fat stomach and a life that got more stillborn every day. The child wanted Rosie, her lavender smell, her floating island and bread pudding . . ."

2

"Nobody in that family wanted Lillie to marry me. I was too dark, I didn't have any money, and I wasn't a teacher, and when she died, they all blamed me for her death . . ." My father's face is full of memory. Sad black eyes brim full of resemblance. Wide shoulders and chest holding the past erect. He is always distracted, always looking behind him. Dead Lillie calls, he runs to her photograph. The disdain of her family lives in his eyes. "They had Lillie engaged to some cousin when I met her; they certainly couldn't see why I came calling. Too dark with nothing but a mortician's certificate from Dexter's Embalming School."

The memory is etched in his mind. He has only to look behind him. The wide circular driveway is there. He drives through the archway in an old black Packard. Stone houses greet him with big screened-in porches. Weeping willows lean in the distance. Dead Lillie waits on the porch: "Momma, Josh Edwards is here!" She runs out to meet him. "You look as spiffy as your car," she says, laughing. "I bolstered myself up the best I knew how," he says with a smile, his black hair well brushed and crinkly. Rosie comes out. "How do you do?" She extends her hand, a breathless fragrance about her. "I have dinner ready and my family is here, will you come in and join us?" The table is set for nine. A dark blue damask cloth. Tall silver candelabras. A profusion of jonquils and daisies. Rosie puts Josh on her right next to Aunt Gert. "You're about to have a rare treat," Aunt Gert says, nudging him. "I've been eating Rosie's cooking since I was five years old, no two meals are ever alike; she whistles over them, blows a little tune while she pats and kneads, you can feel her pretty fingers on everything . . ." They nod in prayer; Uncle Justin begins, "This is the food from our own hands, we respect that we grew it, we respect that we prepared it, we give thanks among ourselves for the strength and foresight that have carried us this far, now we ask that You turn Your pity and attention to those who need it. Serve me some of that soup, Rosie," and he holds out his bowl. "I can never let out a good amen after one of your prayers, Justin," Aunt Anna remarks.

"I feel like we just sent the Man away when He was about to settle down for a good meal." "I didn't send Him away, I didn't invite Him," Uncle Justin grunts. "He's always welcome at my table," Rosie offers, "if He likes leek soup," and she claps her hands. "Atta girl, Rosie," Uncle Jethro grunts. They sip their soup. Josh watches. A conspicuous stranger hardly daring to eat.

"What an awesome pile of flesh they were . . . all bloodless and anemic looking, sitting around Rosie's table like some fashionable coterie of ghosts . . ."

His eyes move around the table. To Aunt Anna, her pallid face lined with moles. To Uncle Justin, skin gleaming like marble. To Rosie, long pale fingers with pretty pink nails. To Uncle Jethro, blind as a bat, with ivory skin and hair like ornaments without a soul. To Aunt Gert, green eyes, amber hair coiled high on her head. To Daddy Jim, a pinch of cinnamon in his skin, a somber grace in his bearing.

"Cousins married to cousins who intermarried again with still other cousins until the blood grew thinner, the skin fairer, the mind weaker, obsessed with one and only one idea . . . keep the race fair at all costs, above all considerations see that the race get fairer and fairer . . ." He shakes his head. ". . . but I loved it . . . Lillie took me all over the place . . . Uncle Justin ran the farm, Daddy Jim had a little carpentry shop, Jethro and your uncle Obie—he's dead now, he used to run a print and machine shop. Rosie had the most beautiful garden, dogwood and magnolia trees, Irish roses and azaleas. It was a private world and I loved it."

3

Three weeks out of every summer the court sent me to Rosie's. My father didn't come inside. Rosie sent Daddy Jim out to pick up me and my things.

"You're home again!" Rosie greeted me, and clapped her hands. Softly. A little elegant clap. She didn't hug me but she was glad to see me. "I made you an orange cake and floating island." We go sit in her kitchen, her long, pale fingers with the pink nails rolling-kneading-patting-tucking while she whistles, short little breaths of a whistle, and talks to me. "We'll have Verta straighten your hair tomorrow, then we'll go see Aunt Gert and Uncle Justin. Uncle Justin will take us to Cape May to see your aunt Anna."

"You got the girl"—Uncle Justin nods—"how come she don't look like Lillie?" and he shakes his head all the way to Cape May.

"How much farther, Uncle Justin?"

"How much farther? Every time the wheels turn,

child, we're a little bit closer, now you sit back and think about that . . . every time the wheels turn we're a little bit closer."

Aunt Anna lives in a little house that smells like the ocean. Dark rocking chairs, gray throw rugs, family pictures in wooden frames.

"Who's that, Aunt Anna?"

"That's your uncle Jethro when he was a boy . . ."

"And who's that?"

"That's your mother . . . Lillie . . . with my Rowena who lives in London . . ."

"And who's that?"

"That's Lillie again, when she finished teachers college."

"And that's you?"

"Yes, that's me with the first class I ever taught at the Cape May Normal School . . . and here's your grandmother, here's Rosie, when she taught domestic science at the Old Ironsides school . . ."

Prim aunts and uncles with bustles and bows. I plot which cousins married which other cousins. I look at dead Lillie. How am I related to her? Sallow skin bleached whiter than flour. Hair bred silky and straighten-free. How am I related to her?

"Eight people at my table," Rosie announces to

Anna, "with chrysanthemums and morning glories for my centerpiece and my green china. We start with my fruit compote—fresh blueberries, strawberries, pineapple, and fresh-grated coconut." Rosie taps the air with her long, pale fingers, enumerating everything. Her chicken à la king in homemade pastry shells, her fresh peas, her dark, delicious devil's food cake, her homemade peach ice cream. Breathless and subtle she captures us, makes us savor her meal. Is it the pout on those little-girl lips, the gray-black sweep of her wonderful curls, the feeling for taste that drips from her skin? What is it? My Rosie, so breathless and subtle with life.

"Rosie Pierson is the most elegant woman I ever knew," my father says, "everything in my life is for her. I raise you for her. I made myself into something for her. She's the most elegant woman I ever knew . . ."

"But you don't speak to each other . . ."

"It doesn't matter, everything I will ever have to say to her I said over Lillie's tomb, I even wrote it down and put it in Lillie's hand before I closed the coffin . . . Lillie knows."

Uncle Justin wakes me up just enough to lift me in his arms and carry me into the house.

"Good night, Rosie, the child's all right. A little colored and that's hard to take, but she follows with her eyes like Lillie used to and that's something . . . I think Josh might amount to a little bit, she says he's already got his teaching certificate and he's still going to school. He'll amount to more than most, but Lillie needed somebody golden and he's sure 'n hell less than that."

Rosie shoos me a good night, then disappears while Daddy Jim slips on my nightie. "Night, child, don't worry, I'll wake you in time . . ." and he hugs me. Daddy Jim will see that I don't wet Rosie's bed. Before dawn he'll lift me in his arms and carry me to the bathroom. He knows I'm afraid I might wet Rosie's bed; he knows and always catches me in time. "Night, child."

He leaves me in the shiny room with the ruffled curtains, the pretty lilac wallpaper. I make up a scene to put me to sleep. I'm holding dead Lillie's hand, and she says to me, "Hello, Lillian, now you can start all over again. I'll take you to Rosie's, to Uncle Justin's and Aunt Anna's, and this time they'll know who you are, now you can start all over again . . ."

4

"Lillie really loved your father," Aunt Gert told me one Fourth of July picnic when all the H_____ clan gathers. "She was crazy about that man . . . The family took one look at him and nearly floated out to sea . . . but I thought he was handsome . . . Nobody else did because they don't like colored looks, but he had handsome colored looks and he stood out. It's true he was scared, but he had other things on his mind: Lillie. He wanted her and she liked it, yes she did, if you ever saw them together you could see it. He was tall, but slight; she was a little on the fleshy side; they fit to each other, not in anybody else's eyes, but I thought they did. Rosie wanted them to wait. Lillie could teach; she had her certificate from the teachers college and Josh could go on and get his degree. But they couldn't wait, and Lillie got pregnant fast and there was no money. Then she got sick early on when she was carrying you. Josh called Rosie to come get her, but Rosie wouldn't do it. Lillie even got on the phone and asked her for money. Lillie couldn't stand not having any money; she loved Josh but she hated the bills, and the bill collectors, and Josh got so few calls to bury people in those days. But Rosie wouldn't come, she just sent a little money. Even when Lillie was in the hospital she wouldn't come, none of them would, not even Uncle Justin who loved her like his own daughter. I went . . . poor Lillie, she had 'fun' written all over her but she took it to the grave . . . it broke your father's heart to know he couldn't give her a thing . . . Rosie should have been there, but Rosie hates sickness and death. I tried to tell Lillie that . . . Rosie likes pretty tables and good food, crepe dresses and nice straw hats . . . Uncle Justin and me raised Lillie more than Rosie did . . . I tried to tell Lillie her mother hated Josh most because he came smelling of death and colored stock and now he wanted her to come see her child in the hospital. She couldn't do that, she just couldn't. I called to tell her Lillie was dead and she hung up on me, and the next time she saw Lillie was at the funeral home. She went up to Josh and asked if she could take care of you. Josh said yes, that she could have you for a while until he could get himself together, then he wanted you back . . ."

5

"You were five months old when Rosie took you, and you were going on three when the court gave you back." My father's face grows dark with memory. "I used to come see you every Sunday, they'd have you dressed up and sitting in that glider when I drove up, you were little and chubby but you never smiled, you never took my hand. I'd ask if you knew who I was, if you knew I was your daddy and one day you'd be coming to live with me, but you just looked at me. Sometimes I'd think I couldn't stand another one of these Sundays. I wasn't allowed in the house once that court business started, but we'd walk around the grounds. I'd stand and look at Rosie's garden. Lillie was there at every turn . . ."

He remembers everything. He has a perfect smell for death and pain, the thousand and one slights that have colored his life, the happiness snatched before he could taste it. He perseveres and remembers.

"When the court gave me custody, Rosie sent you home in a red-and-white polka-dot dress. Daddy Jim carried you out to the car and put you on the front seat. 'Good-bye, child,' he said . . . and you looked at him and you didn't cry, you didn't say a word. He and I shook hands and I brought you home."

And it was dark. And did the house smell of dead flowers? And did I walk in my sleep, find you in the darkness falling down on your knees: ". . . I have the child now, Lillie, she's here in this house and I'll raise her from now on . . ."?

"I thought I'd made a terrible mistake. You didn't speak. I'd ask if you knew I was your daddy and that's why you were here with me, and you just looked at me. You did whatever I asked, you were very well-behaved, but you didn't speak. I thought, This child will never love me, it doesn't even know who I am, why did I think I had a right to it? I thought I'd have to give you back and I made up my mind I couldn't keep you if you weren't happy, no siree, I couldn't keep waking you up every morning and getting nothing, no good mornings, no hugs, not even a smile. I couldn't stand much more, I was going to call Rosie even if it broke me for good; I was going to call and tell her to come get you. 'I think you should go back to Rosie's,' I said to you . . . We were sitting at this very table, I was giving you your breakfast. 'I don't think you like your daddy,' I said, 'I think you miss Daddy Jim and Rosie . . .' and I started to cry . . . I just went all to pieces . . . 'And whether you like me or not I've got to keep you . . .' That's the last time I ever thought about giving you up . . ."

6

Mornings at Rosie's come in shiny and new. The floors smell of pinecones. When I take my bath, I'm inside a blue-and-white bubble the scent of lavender, the feel of round lemon soaps that melt in my palm. The sun is all over this shiny little house.

"I made you sweetbreads, Lillian"—Rosie claps her hands—"creamed sweetbreads on toasted Englishes, that's our breakfast." She moves about her kitchen, cutting, slicing, stirring, mixing, whistling in short little breaths while she talks. "And have you seen my nasturtiums? Go take a peek, child, we'll go out later and give everything a little drink, but here . . . take the scissors . . . bring us a few for our table . . . Make us a centerpiece, child, something fresh and full of morning to go with our breakfast."

I wish I could hug Rosie, her kitchen smells of puddings and pies, roasts and sweetbreads, hot rolls and clam chowder; her garden has the hot scent of lilac and myrrh.

"Did you tell Rosie I'm a teacher now?" my father asks.

"Of course I did . . ."

"And what did she say to that?"

"She clapped her hands."

"And did you tell her I'll have my doctorate in a few years?"

"Of course I did . . ."

"And what did she say to that?"

"She said, 'Oh, that's very nice, that's very nice indeed.'"

"The first time your father came to this house," Rosie says to me at breakfast, "I made sliced rare steak that melted like butter, roasted potatoes with mushrooms, string beans, and an orange cake every bit as good as the one you been gobbling since you got here. He had on a tan suit that was well tailored, too, and my Lillie showed him off like the man of the hour. He had two strikes against him right away: he buried the dead, and my Lillie was already courting a distant cousin of your uncle Jethro's who was a teacher at the Old Ironsides Normal School. His name was Randolph. Your father had more energy than Randolph, but your father was also scared. I saw that, but Lillie didn't. Lillie already had her degree. He didn't have a thing. I hold it against him that he married her without having a thing. But I'm not surprised he's amounted to something; he had energy, anybody could see that."

Afternoons at Rosie's I play in the swamp, pretend I'm falling into quicksand, black moccasins are chasing me, arrows are rifling through the air. Afternoons at Rosie's I come back wet and muddy, Daddy Jim plops me in the silver washtub and scrubs me down. He never says a word, but he hugs me often while he dries me, slips on clean clothes, and sends me inside to Rosie's for lunch. "We'll have tea sandwiches with chicken salad, Lillian, some nice deviled eggs, a tall glass of apricot nectar, and floating island for dessert." I'm spanking clean, pleased and happy to be sitting in Rosie's kitchen.

"Did you tell Rosie about the house?" my father asks.

"Of course I did."

"And the big rooms we've got and the yard? Did you tell her about my roses?"

"Everything, my room with the new wallpaper, the dining room with the oak furniture, everything."

"And what did she say?"

"She whistled . . ."

"Your father's the oddest man I ever knew," Rosie says to me at lunch, "he won't sit still long enough to die, he keeps moving. Nothing can hold him down, he'll have everything he thinks he wants . . ."

Evenings at Rosie's are full of games. Pinochle, bridge, canasta, whist. Poached salmon and asparagus for dinner, fresh rhubarb pie for dessert.

"Do they think you're well-mannered?" my father asks.

"I think so . . ."

"And what do they say about that?"

"Rosie claps her hands, Daddy Jim smiles."

"One thing I have to say about your father," Rosie says to me while we're playing cards. "He's the best bridge partner I ever had, he can bid a hand for exactly what it's worth and bring it in on time . . ."

I wish I could hug Rosie. Everything about her is soft and grand. But she will not let me hug her. What kind of granddaughter did you want, Rosie? A sleek, prim child with shiny hair? How did I get here, skin too dark, hair mixed up? How did dead Lillie ever manage such a thing?

"Does Daddy Jim ever talk?" I once asked my father.

"Not in all the years I went to that house. Rosie talks. The house smiles, and Rosie talks. Daddy Jim nods his head."

7

Sand dunes. Windy sun. Picnic tables. Massive waves breaking in the distance. Clusters of ivory women in straw hats. I'm sitting beside Rosie. Uncle Justin's across from me, looking in my eyes for signs of dead Lillie. Aunt Lou Lou comes over with my cousin Jocelyn.

"Hello, Rosie, I see you have Lillian again this summer . . . How are you, Lillian? You've grown, it's nice to see you again," her prim nasal voice intones. "I brought Jocelyn over, Rosie, I thought the girls could play while we grown-ups chitchat." She smiles through starched cheeks puffy as clouds, dark red hair in a skintight bun. I hate Aunt Lou Lou. I don't know why. I just hate Aunt Lou Lou.

"She's a creepy piece of flesh, all right," my father says. "I don't know which one of Rosie's brothers or sisters got her here, but it's my guess she got bred between them . . ."

"You want to play Scrabble?" cousin Jocelyn asks in the same blanched tone.

"All right," I answer, proud of all the games Rosie's taught me. We find a table and start to play. Rosie brings us deviled eggs, a mound of tea sandwiches made with chicken salad, creamed cheese and olives, a full pitcher of apricot punch.

"You can make the first word," cousin Jocelyn says.

"*R-E-V-I-V-A-L*." And I used all seven letters.

"That's pretty good," and she makes a six-letter word to cross it: BOVINE.

"I know what that means," I say. "Rosie taught me that word. It means sluggish, dull, like an ox or a cow."

"Lillian, come meet your cousin Rowena, she's just back from London."

The pallid lady of Aunt Anna's photograph.

"Hello, Lillian. Oh, I knew your mother well, she and I were the closest of all the cousins. How are you, child?" Her voice sings and she gives me the brightest smile.

"Rowena was Lillie's best friend," my father says. "She had spunk, went off to London to become an actress. She wasn't as pretty as Lillie, but she had the most wonderful voice, just like you were gliding along. What's she like now?"

Rowena takes my hand, and we go for a walk along the beach. "Oh, we had some good, good times, your mother and I did. Did you know your mother was very funny? She's the one who thought up all the good pranks and I just went along. 'Oh, Lillie,' I'd say, 'we're going to get in so much trouble, Uncle Justin's going to kill us if he finds out.' But you couldn't stop Lillie, she had lots of nerve. I have a whole rhyme book I'll show you, full of couplets she made up about everybody, Aunt Gert, Uncle Justin, Rosie . . . everybody's in it . . . she could think of the sharpest things to say . . ."

"You loved my mother . . ."

"I did . . . I did . . ." She begins to cry.

Then I see dead Lillie. All at once she's as clear as day. She has the brightest smile. Full plump arms that sweep me to her. I am suddenly real. I can touch myself.

"Why did she die?"

"Oh, child, I wish I could answer that . . ."

8

In the mornings my father stops at my room: "Lillian, it's time to get up." Then I hear him turn on the shower. He talks to himself: "No siree, you won't live to see that day . . . Of course I'd like that job, it'd be a godsend. I could sell the business, send the child to private school . . . but you won't live to see the day I get it that way, no siree . . ." He runs past my room naked, holding a towel against his private parts. Dead Lillie watches me while he reads his *Daily Word*, says his morning prayers. When I hear him go downstairs I go into his room. Dead Lillie watches me sniff his cologne, open his drawers, where dozens of black socks are kept in neat balls, where there are garters and sleeveless undershirts, white boxer shorts and shirts stiff from the laundry. I play with his keys, take the shoe trees in and out of his shoes, count his neckties, rearrange them on the silver ring. I apologize to dead Lillie for smelling his room, for sniffing about in his things. I stare at her. The round full face. The dark eyes that never tell me a thing. I walk backward away from her and go downstairs.

There is scrapple cooking, toast and fried eggs. He's still talking to himself: ". . . no siree, and the real crux of the matter nobody wants to deal with, that's the thing that gets to you . . ." He serves my food. "We're going to the Met this Friday, I've got standing-room tickets. We'll eat out, and next Friday I'd like to take you to the philharmonic." He's always distracted but I'm included in the sweep of his mind.

He goes back to his sifting: "And I told old man Watkins that the only way I'd take that job is when it's offered to me as fair and square as it's offered to anyone else with my credentials, yes siree . . ."

He looks spiffy. His crinkly black hair is combed to the side. He sports a gray suit with a bow tie. Black shoes that shine. He looks clean. Righteous. Dominant. "Yes, sir, there's a certain order to things, and that's what I respect. I don't think anyone'll ever live to see the day Josh Edwards turns his back on what he sees as the fit way to do something. No, sir, you can place your bets on that one . . ."

At night he braids my hair. He brushes it hard. His heavy hands pull it tight from my scalp and plait it in four harsh braids. It hurts. "We can make something out of your hair. It won't ever be as straight as Lillie's, but we can make something out of it." He scrubs my face, washes my ears, puts out my clothes for the next day.

"Night, child, try not to wet your bed."

"How did dead Lillie die?"

"She got pleurisy, then meningitis . . . they couldn't do a thing . . ."

"Did she ever see me?"

He can't recall: "I don't know, I know she went into a coma soon after the delivery, then we brought you home. I was going back and forth a lot. Then Rosie took you . . .

"She only came out of the coma one time, and the only person she asked for was Rosie . . ."

He looks over my shoulder at something. Is it dead Lillie in her hospital bed? Is it Rosie at the funeral home?

"Aunt Gert pretended that Rosie was on her way. I sat at the foot of the bed waiting for her to recognize me . . ."

He looks over my shoulder at something. Is it dead Lillie staring at his face? Is it Aunt Gert begging Rosie to come?

"I don't think she ever did see you, Lillian, I can't remember when she could have . . ."

9

Daddy Jim just died. I go with my father to Rosie's. She sits by the window crying. "My Lillie's gone, and now my Jim's gone . . ." She looks at us.

"Hello, Rosie," my father says. "You know how much I thought of Daddy Jim. I couldn't not come."

He looks around and smiles. He's home. He's at Rosie's again and he's home. "I think the house could use a little straightening up, Rosie. People will be coming. Do you have any food prepared?"

He begins to pick up her things. Her silk nightgown thrown across the bed with her dressing gown.

He lifts them carefully and hangs them in the closet. He makes her bed, pulls the sheets crisp, pounds her large French pillows into shape, drapes her pretty satin quilt perfectly in place.

"Lillian, help me with the dusting, now, and we'll give the floors a quick once-over, too."

He moves from room to room, straightening, polishing, dusting, talking to himself.

"Should I make a cake?" Rosie asks him.

"If you feel up to it, I think that's a good idea . . ."

She gets up and he follows her down to the kitchen.

"How are your geraniums doing?" I hear him ask. "You know, I planted some nasturtiums this spring, but the thing you've got to see are my roses—they're every color in the rainbow, Rosie. I go out in my yard, I can't believe the spectacle that greets me . . ."

They begin to talk about the funeral.

"You got old man Newcombe, I hope . . . he's the only decent undertaker in these parts. Now what suit are you putting him in? I better go upstairs and pick one out, and a nice tie, too. We'll have him looking just like himself, Rosie."

I hear him in Daddy Jim's closet: ". . . yes, sir, and when things feel right you have to do them . . . Why she was just sitting there and it was the right time . . . yes, sir, when I walked through that door I knew it was the right time . . ."

He lays Daddy Jim's dark blue pin-striped suit on the bed, picks out clean underwear, a nice light blue shirt, and a bow tie. He steps back and surveys his choices. "He'll look just fine in that. Now, where are his cuff links and his watch? And I wonder what Rosie wants to do about his wedding ring . . ."

He puts in a call to Newcombe, the undertaker: "Mr. Newcombe, Josh Edwards on the phone, Rosie Pierson's son-in-law. That's right. Now, we have his things all ready for you. No, I'm sure Rosie would prefer a morning funeral, you set the wake for tomorrow night, that's right. And an eleven o'clock service the following morning. Now, when your men have finished embalming him, give me a call . . . I'd like to see the body before Rosie does . . ."

He puts in a call to the florist: "Josh Edwards on the phone, Mrs. Rosie Pierson's son-in-law . . . that's right . . . You may have heard by now that my father-in-law just passed away . . . that's right . . . thank you very much . . . Now, I'd like to order three large sprays, one from his wife, one from his son-in-law, and one from his granddaughter, that's right . . . Now, let me tell you exactly what I want in each arrangement . . ."

He remembers everything. The kind of sermon the minister should preach. The hymns the choir should sing. The words of the eulogy that Rosie must read. The number of friends who should speak. He remembers everything. Even dead Lillie will have her say:

Did ever a girl have a father
As dear and as sweet as my Jim.
His love is as wide as a river,
Why, it never can come to an end.
It's he who remembers to tuck me in
And kiss me a long good night.
And he's never grouchy or grumpy
And has no taste at all for a fight.

He remembers everything. "Now, Rosie, what do you want to do about food?" His sad black eyes are wide and crisp. His lips are compressed to a seal. What next, Rosie? they ask. What's the next thing I must do?

Rosie takes out her little notebook and makes a shopping list. She enumerates everything. Creamed spinach and mushrooms. Spoon bread and homemade rolls. Broiled tomatoes and string beans. Capon and wild duck. She enumerates everything.

"Does that sound like a fine little meal?" she asks, and claps her hands. Softly. An elegant little clap.

ABOUT THE AUTHOR

© DOUGLAS COLLINS

Kathleen Collins was a pioneer African American
playwright, filmmaker, civil rights activist,
film editor, and educator. Her film *Losing Ground*
is one of the first features made by a black woman
in America, and is an extremely rare
narrative portrayal of a black female intellectual.
Collins died in 1988 at the age of forty-six.
www.kathleencollins.org